¿Friends?

A story to bring awareness

C. H. Magical

C. H. Magical

Book Cover by Maja Kopunovic

Contents

For all those who have scars, no one sees. For the ones who are on the ledge. You are not alone and you are loved.

FOR AN IMMERSIVE READING experience, I recommend listening to the following songs in the suggested chapter to get a better feel for the characters and the chapter's content.

****

"Sara" - We Three
"No time to die" - Billie Eilish

Uncertain

"Through the dark" - One direction
"I know your Secrets" - Tommee Profitt, Liv Ash

Squire

"Cool for the Summer" - Demi Lovato
"Made you Look" - Meghan Trainor

The Party

"Bang Bang" - Ariana Grande, Jessie J, and Nicki Minaj
"Caught in the Fire" - Klergy

Popular

"Limit" - Citizen Soldier
"Don't deserve you" - Plumb

Summer

"Empire State Mind" - Alicia Keys
"Searching" - KVDE

Secrets

"House with no mirrors," - Sasha Sloan

"100 Bandaids" - Faouzia
Eyes of the Truth
"Can you hold me" - NF, Britt Nicole
"Head above water" - Avril Lavigne
Someone New
"Freedom" - Kygo, Zak Abel
"Bring me to life" - Evanescence
Betrayal by a Friend
"All I need" - Within Temptation
"Broken Girl" - Matthew West
Confession
"Anyone but Me" - Citizen Soldier
"How do I say Goodbye" - Dean Lewis
Shattered
"Hush" - HELLYEAH
"Skyfall" - Adele
Mother's Grief
"Fallen Angel" - Three Days Grace
"Can you feel my heart" - Bring Me The Horizon
Consequences
"You don't know," - Katelyn Tarver
"Apologize" - One Republic
Horrifying Truths
"Girls like us" - Zoe Wess
"Your power" - Billie Eilish
Love?
"Everything is Lost" - Maggie Eckford
"Till it happens to you" - Lady Gaga.
Brave
"Back from the dead," - KVDE and J-Ryz
"Hold on" - Chord Overstreet
Fallen Angel
"Train Wreck" - James Arthur
"I can only imagine" - MercyMe
Grace Wins
"Girl on Fire," - Alicia Keys

SHE WAS MY BEST friend.

How could she do this to me? Betray me... I thought our friendship was forever. We swore it. Sealed it with a pinky promise when we were kids. Yet it seems our vow only meant something to me...

Otherwise, I wouldn't be alone and broken. Being assaulted left and right. A punching bag that no one is willing to catch when it collapses but throw away.

I thought I knew her... I opened up to her about my demons, my every doubt and fear... I completely trusted her. I believed she would forever be there for me. The only one who would remain by my side, no matter what.

Be there rain or sun. Clear skies or thunderstorms. But I was wrong; I trusted the wrong person, and it hurts so much.

Why did she have to lie to me? Hide her true feelings and who she was? Deceive me in such a way that would finally drown me in my despair...

What did I ever do to her? What did I do that drove her to ruin my life so viciously?

I wish I knew so I could go back in time and remedy whatever hurt her. Fix what I did wrong. So, I would have never lost her to begin with. Her betrayal is killing me from the inside out, and I don't have it in me to keep fighting. I'm tired, so tired of fighting to simply breathe.

I don't want to think or feel her betrayal anymore. It torments my heart far too much. She knows the truth, yet she still lets everyone sputter lies and warp the truth of my story. Condemning me further into the hell I already know and creating a new one for me at school.

Robbing me of any haven free of pain.

And I don't want to keep worrying. Looking over my shoulder. Not at home and not at school. I don't want to fear anyone anymore. I just want to be free and know peace. I want the pain to stop...

Mom will be okay. She'll have *him* and my siblings. Dad's already gone and I'll get to see him again. And I lost Becca a long time ago, the moment she went to that stupid populars' party. Brad will forget about me quickly. After all, I'm no one. Nothing more than a burden on everyone else.

They will be okay. Better without me. I won't be missed.

I need the tears to cease. The pain to become numb. I don't want to... to... I don't want to keep breathing. Not when it hurts so much.

I don't want to live.

My soul craves peace. One only death can provide. I need everything to stop. The voices, the bullying, the abuse. I want to be free.

No one cares for me anymore. They won't miss me. Everyone will be better off without me, like those stupid sites say.

Their hateful words come back to haunt me and drown me even further in the spiral of dark thoughts. It's as if they were all right here with me, yelling them at me. I cradle my knees to my chest as I pull on my hair, needing them all to shut up. Needing the madness of my hell to disappear.

But it doesn't. It further grows. Ignoring it is nowhere near in mind. Because it's impossible to do so. I'm not strong enough.

The feeling of ending it all only grows even further. I should just listen to those who seek my death. They're right,

I'm nothing but a terrible human being. I should just end it all and be done with it.

I once thought I had Becca by my side, but even she left me in the end. Betrayed me for them. Left me behind to be in the spotlight and be... normal. Something I'll never be. I'm far too broken.

Tears blur my vision to no end as they pour out of me like a fragmented dam as I contemplate my options for escaping this world permanently. The dark void inside pulling me underneath its beautiful promise of death.

I don't want to go to school tomorrow just to be tortured with their lies and fists. I don't want to endure another night or moment in his presence, or worse underneath his heavy body. I can't do this anymore.

My only escape is to disappear... disappear into the darkness to escape the pain that consumes me daily. The price is far too high this time around and I can't bear it. I'm tired of being the one to pay for the broken plates.

That's the only answer to my problems. My only escape to the pain that has me in a tight hold, unwilling to let me go. Death. So, I won't have to endure another day in this hell. My only way out is to stop breathing.

End my life.

I'll just be ridding the world of its error. Having been born. It just brought everyone far more pain and death than I'm worth. I'm a mistake and I need to correct it. My tears will cease and I'll be at peace. Who cares if my heart stops beating in the process? No one has cared for me before and they won't now.

¿FRIENDS?

Goodbye, cruel world, you're finally getting your wish. I'll cease to live and a blunder will be fixed, how it should have been from the start.

Uncertain

♥

2 Years Earlier

Cassie and Becca were seated outside the covered area at the front of their school as they awaited their parents to pick them up as after-school activities had ended for the day. Yet both friends shared very distinct feelings about the entire ordeal. Cassie, who avoided going home like the plague, out of fear for the monster that lived in her home, absolutely dreaded the moment they arrived. On the other hand, Becca was impatient for their arrival after such a long day of school, making up for the days she had already missed.

Yet despite her excitement to go home, one glance towards her best friend and seeing the telltale signs of her fear had those feelings crushing her heart. Seeing her playing with the rings on her fingers and the nervous tapping of her foot against the concrete, along with the shifting to nail biting and occasional hair play, had her wishing that she didn't know what they meant. Sentiments of guilt churned in her stomach as it swirled with waves of compassion at the very thought.

She knew of Cassie's terror of being home and the reasons. Being her confidant made her privy to the knowledge of the hell her friend lived and, as much as she sometimes hated it, there were times she sought to be ignorant of it all. Her friend's horrors broke her heart, but sometimes her friend's torment undermined the problems that arose in her life. It didn't matter that Cassie tried to be there as much as possible for her because the simple knowledge of knowing dampened their conversations.

But even then, she would always stand by her side. They'd been friends since they were three, and that meant something to them both. Where even the thought of not being there for one another was an inconceivable thought that neither of them would dare harbor. They protected one another and confided everything to each other. All but one thing.

Becca's long-time love for popular guy Hugh Squire, the brother of her best friend's bully. But fearing her best friend's reaction and thinking he would never show interest in her, she kept it a secret. Instead, she focused on being there for her as much as possible.

They were inseparable.

Right until Cassie began dating Hugh Squire two months prior. Betrayal never sunk so deep and heartbreak never felt so raw. So Becca focused her attention on another goal because hating Cassandra seemed like such a foul move when she didn't know of her feelings and she suffered so much.

Sadly, her heart set on becoming both like the guy she loved and her friend's bully to heal; popular.

Cassie

Drawing out a sigh and tapping my foot nervously, I wait for Becca to return from the bathroom while everyone around me is engaged in meaningless conversations like normal people. Something I wish I had, but that'll never be me. I'm far too broken and I'm okay with it just being us.

I don't need anyone but Becca, anyway.

Quality over quantity and she's everything to me.

My heart gnaws over the huge void I've felt separating us ever since I accepted to be Hugh's girlfriend. A choice I now regret seeing how strained my friendship with Becca has become in two short months. Truthfully, being with him isn't worth it, but how can I break his heart and say goodbye to someone who offers me more time outside of my hell?

Another sigh parts from me as grief floods me and images of what awaits me at home plays like a merry-go-round. Goosebumps run rampant over my skin, and I shake my head to clear my negative thoughts. Mom gave me permission to go to Becca's house today.

I have a few more hours and by tomorrow I'll be at my dad's place. Free of lecherous hands to violent ones. I can handle one night and the clock has still not run out.

My hands run over my face and scrub away the terror to focus on the now instead of what's coming. A shaky breath leaves me as panic weighs heavily on my chest like the bitch she is. *I'm at school and safe for now.*

Drawing deep breaths, I run a hand over the warm piece of metal around my neck to ground myself from the memories. Instantly, my brain shifts from thinking of the monster and evil witch to my best friend. And just like that, I think once more of her and Hugh.

Resolution fills me as I ponder between them both.

It doesn't matter what he offers; he isn't Becca and he could never replace her. She comes first and I can live without him. If it comes down to them both, then the choice is simple.

A shudder runs down my body at the thought, but I'm determined to follow through with it. I clutch the straps of my backpack to settle my hands in a nervous tic I've picked up while thinking of the feelings I've developed for Hugh. He isn't like Jenine, his sister, or my tormentor, and I'm growing to like him.

I'll talk to Becca today and then leave him if need be.

Shifting my weight from foot to foot, I scan the surrounding crowd in search of her. Yet something gnaws at the back of my mind. A feeling that I'm missing a vital piece of information and I crave to know the answer.

But the moment my eyes catch sight of perfect auburn curls that perfectly fall over gentle shoulders; it all goes away. There she is; my best friend. A smile tugs at the corners of my lips and I take a step forward, only for it to fall at the new perspective that greets me.

Becca isn't alone. No, she's chatting with a group of people with a carefree grin.

What is she doing talking to the populars? We detest them, so why is she speaking to them?

They're spoiled rotten human beings who have no regard for who they hurt. They own the school and thrive on making everyone else's life a living hell. People who have mocked us in the past, me more than her, but the fact remains they are our bullies.

So, why is my best friend indulging them in conversation when they don't deserve it? Do her notions to become popular involve her befriending the very ones who saw glee in our tears? No, it couldn't be.

Surely, she knows I remain the butt of their jokes even if it's not as much as before I began dating Hugh, but still she has to know. I know I don't complain much about them anymore, having become used to it by now and their pranks and words are easier to handle, unlike the monster and evil witch, but still. Becca has to know they still hurt and wouldn't go about being friends with them.

Her head falls back as she laughs at something being said, as if it were the most humorous thing she's heard and it's a stab to my fragile heart. I take a step back as if I've been struck by the evil witch at the sight. She looks so joyous and carefree, like everyone else. Normal even.

A frog gets caught in my throat as I ponder if maybe the

problem isn't everyone else but me. Because why else would I be everyone's punching bag but her? There has to be a reason.

Life is a constant cycle of pain where beggars can't be choosers. I know that, but for once I would like to be free of its cruelties. It's not amiss to me that I'm asking for too much once again, but how I wish I could be free of them just once. Watching Becca with the populars has my soul writhing in agony as it screams out, yet my lips remain sealed.

She's the one true thing I truly have, and it feels like I'm losing her.

I know I'll never be normal and I'm far too broken for that. But Becca is the only lifeboat I have in the sea of despair. Something I wish to be for her, too. The thought of losing her to those people has me slipping underneath the water once more.

I stand there like an idiot, feeling displaced and alone, unable to pull my eyes away before getting caught. But it's too late by the time I'm able to surpass my shock as her head swivels towards me and all their eyes land on me. I shift uncomfortably under the scrutiny of their gazes, feeling exposed and all too aware of the glee that had enveloped them now gone.

Jenine rattles something off to Becca before glaring at me with the most condescending look I've ever seen. She grimaces before turning on her heels and walking away with her posse. I wish I knew why they... why Jenine hated me so much.

A breath of relief escapes me at the sight of them leaving while Becca stands there for a second before finally walking over to me. It kills me to see her earlier expression be replaced with a tired and somber look. Is that what I bring out in her? Am I the villain and I've never noticed?

"So, what did Jenine and her minions want?" I force the question out with an uncertain smile I pray passes off as easygoing while clutching the straps of my backpack. My eyes divert to those around us and focus on people watching as if it were my second nature. But at this point, I suppose it is.

I allow the mask I grant everyone else to fall into place, not wanting to drag her down.

"Nothing, just inviting me to one of the AMAZING parties they throw," she says with beads of excitement bleeding into her tone despite her apparent attempt to disguise it. Shock shakes me at my core as my gaze flies to her as fast as a whip to be met with twinkling eyes and a small smile on her face. Disbelief pours through my insides.

"What? You know they hate us!" I try for a calm tone, but my anxiety betrays me as it comes out in a screech. Close to yelling. The one thing I avoid. "They have to be up to something, Becks!" I mumble with a racing heart. My nerves fried as I see a heap of red flags she appears oblivious to.

She can't go. They'll do something to her or use her to hurt me. I can't...

They are always up to no good, especially when it concerns me. Jenine has always done everything in her power to make my life at school hell, and she always will. I know she'll never change, nor does she have redeeming qualities. Becca has to know that. She knows everything.

"Just because you don't like them doesn't mean they're up to something, Cassie," she replies in a vacant tone. "I'm going to go."

She says it as if going to their party was nothing. But it's not nothing, it's everything. Becca isn't gullible enough for their parlor tricks, right?

Feelings of hurt and betrayal with anger being the glue that binds them together take a hold of my heart. She's not even considering it. She's made her mind up to go and I know there is no steering her away from it. But how can she be okay with going with everything they've done to others, to her... to me?

I'm her best friend. Doesn't that count as something?

Best friends have each other's backs. Support one another and take a stand against bullies together. Is this not her betraying our friendship, or am I overreacting yet once again?

"Just because they didn't invite you doesn't mean I can't go," she snaps at me. "I would think you would be happy for me seeing how I want to be popular, but I guess that's too much to ask from my best friend."

My heart stings at her words and the visible hurt in her eyes. My question already answered for me. One relationship grows a void and a party invitation has a wedge being grown between us.

I have to mend it. Jenine and her clique won't take her away from me. Becca and I are stronger than her. If Beks wants to go to this party to achieve her dream of popularity, then I'll support her. She's been there for me through everything and I can be okay with this one thing I don't like.

I can't push her on this or I risk losing her.

"You're right," I say, refraining the tears and forcing a smile. "This might be your chance to popularity like you want," I acknowledge with difficulty.

Popularity is her dream. A new one, but her dream nonetheless. Why? I don't know, but I have to wonder if that's because my focus has always been on surviving, not gaining the favor of those around me. They all pose a threat to hurt me.

"How about we go shopping for a brand-new outfit for this party?" I offer before I end up losing myself in the rabbit hole of my broken thoughts.

Not everyone is broken, and some actually lead normal lives or are able to do normal things like those seen on TV. I need to quit projecting myself onto everyone else. I need to stop feeling sorry for myself.

"I can't," she replies, shaking her head with a glint of sadness in her eyes. "I don't have..."

"Don't worry about it. I got you covered. I'll pay," I add to ease her worries.

She would do the same thing for me if the roles were reversed.

Besides, I'm lucky enough to have a dad who is somewhat well off to give me a credit card and a mom who gives me cash when she can. So, if I can help her with this, then so be it. If only money could solve all my troubles or give me enough courage to leave and run away.

But I don't because I have her. She gives me the courage to keep going and be strong. To avoid seeking the easy way out or falling for addictions.

"Thank you, Cass," she says with a smile and an embrace that feels like normality, safety, and family. She's my sister by heart, and I honestly don't know what would be of me without her. Being the only person I broke my silence to and know will forever have my back.

"Where and when is this party?" I ask with joy at the mending of cracks I can already feel. Hopefully, this is the first step to getting our friendship to what it once was.

"Jenine's house and tonight," she replies with excitement and I nod in acknowledgment, hiding my dislike and current hate for Jenine.

"Well then, let's go, we don't want you to get later than fashionable late to this party," I say, linking our arms, as I spot her grandmother's car.

It feels like normal times and that grants my soul a breath that I haven't felt for a while. Perhaps I may not need to leave Hugh. Maybe I can have them both?

A smile graces my lips the rest of the afternoon as I share laughs with my best friend and we gossip as if we were both normal teenagers. Finding her the perfect outfit in no time and buying other things for the sheer joy of the moment. Eating at the food court and talking about her while waiting for her grandma to pick us up. Even offering to help her get ready, to which she agreed.

It was absolutely blissful even if I felt Jenine was up to something, but I trust Becca to handle herself if need be.

She's holding me together right now, and if I lost her, I would die without a doubt. I can't have her thinking I want to sabotage her dream.

My best friend was ready within an hour and twenty minutes after the clock came to an end. My bubble burst with a simple text. 'I'm outside' simple words that wreaked havoc in me, but I hid it from Becks so she could enjoy her night. With her promise to tell me all the details of how her night goes.

Smiled my way through it with my mom as we spoke about my day as she drove us home... Remained silent during family dinner... Wrote in my diary all about my feelings regarding Becca and this party.

I'm making a big deal over nothing, a storm in a glass of water. Becca and I are stronger than Jenine and whatever games she wants to play.

Right until my bedroom door opened later that night, and the lock was flipped on while my brain blanked to survive what was to come while my mom showered and my siblings slept in their own rooms.

Squire

Jenine

LIKABILITY HAS NOTHING TO do with popularity and everything to do with the heart. But it's something I've never had. Unlike popularity, the one thing I've always had because of the desire I awaken in people.

Therefore, it's been my everything since the first moment I've gotten a taste for it. It's my own personal drug. One I never plan to renounce. It's the only thing I have and to give it up...

Unthinkable.

Popularity will always be mine and I will crush whoever gets in my way. Hell, I'll make it my personal mission to destroy all those who have even a drop of what I have or that which I don't but desperately want.

Just like Cassandra Castillo. The girl who has the mother I can only wish I had. The girl who swept in and stole my best friend before I could even establish a conversation. The girl that has the potential to catch the eyes of my subjects and, worst of all, my popularity.

Bitch, already caught the eye of my brother when they couldn't be any more different. Of all the girls he could have set his eyes on, he has to choose the one girl I utterly hate, fucking typical. But what am I to expect from the golden boy of the family who can do no wrong in our parents' eyes because he has no defects?

Unlike me.

Their daughter, who got disowned the moment they caught her messing around with a girl in her bedroom. How I curse the day they found out that I'm not as straight as they want me to be. Only directing a word my way to know I hold my title and when I bring a boy to them.

But nothing I do compares to the attention I once got to them before that day. I really wish they never found out that I'm bisexual. Maybe then I would still hold their love.

Perhaps then I wouldn't have to recruit to useless diets and empty the contents of my stomach into a toilet. I wouldn't be going to extreme lengths to look as flawless as I do for a single compliment that never comes from them. Hell, they hardly ever notice me at times.

Choosing to travel and only reach out to my brother to express their unwavering love and grant our every wish. But what good does it do to have everything when your own parents hardly acknowledge your existence for the sole reason that you like girls too?

"Jen, where do you want the kegs?" Craig, one of the many guys I've been under in attempts to recover my parents' love, questions me. I quirk an eyebrow at the flirty smirk he throws my way, and my finger points to the corner of the room.

"I see the party is coming along," Hugh voices coming up next to me and I nod, not fully acknowledging him with my sole attention as I inspect every corner of the room. Making sure my party as always forms perfection and envy. It wouldn't be a Jenine Squire's popular party if it didn't.

"Did you ever doubt me, *brother*?" I question, unable to keep the bite off my tone.

"Never, popularity is in our name, Jeni," he comments, impassive as always to my scalding attitude. If only he were the same way to Cassandra's charms. Hell, if only he had set his eyes on Becca Jones instead of the goody two shoes who deems herself above the rest of us to even direct words with anybody.

Once again, I'm questioning what my idiot brother saw in the irritable fly I will crush, eventually. It's just a matter of time. Had only Becca been in his sights, my plan to destroy her would already be in motion and I would have the accomplice I've always wanted.

Because one thing is certain, Cassandra Castillo does not deserve Becca. No, Becky deserves so much better. Someone like me.

"Tell me something I don't know, Squire, and I know you meant to say popularity is my name. You're simply an annex to MY name," I correct him with a smile as slowly my house is converted into exactly what I want it to be. The center of all talk and the want of being present.

"Whatever you say, sister. You damn well know everyone will bend over backward to either be my friend or lover," he says with a light chuckle that grates my nerves.

"Really? Finally, got someone underneath you, or are you still going through a dry spell?"

Through my peripheral vision, I can see his features morph into something resembling anger, but it's like water to my skin. I know he can't touch me and would never dare to begin with. He isn't that type of person.

Without a word, he turns on his heels and storms away.

So freaking predictable.

Rolling my eyes, I watch Grazella put out the wrong color cups. Clearly, I have to do everything. For such a pretty face and lover, she really knows nothing about perfection.

Why I like her is beyond me. Even Craig has better sense than her. Maybe it's time to cut her loose and seek someone else to keep my bed warm.

And maybe while I'm at it, I can help my Hugh out. Becca is coming to this party, after all. How could she not when she's my guest of honor? Perhaps it's time I give him a helping hand and get exactly what I want.

To destroy Cassandra Castillo and call Becca Jones my best friend, as it should have always been.

The Party

Becca

THE THRILL OF BEING invited to Jenine's party made it my priority, despite Cassie not wanting me to go. But I also know she would never forbid me from going. Not everyone can be good at school and stay out of trouble like her. It exhausts me that she tries to change me into something I'm not.

School, books, and studying are her. Parties, drinking, and having fun are me. But then I guess that's why we're best friends, because we're polar opposites. She's there for me and I'm there for her.

Still, it kills me to see her with Hugh when I've loved him for so long, so I put distance between us. It hurts to be away from her, but I can't bring myself to tell her about my feelings for him. And I can't hate her for not seeing it when being home is hell for her.

I lost my dad but still have my grandparents and mom. None of them would ever lay a hand on me like her wicked stepmother, nor sexually assault me like the monster she calls stepdad. Although I'm certain it's progressed to rape, she simply hasn't brought herself to admit it to me and I hate admitting that I truly don't want to know.

Knowing and not being able to do anything is its own

personal hell.

But tonight, I get to go out and have fun to forget that my dad is gone because of a misunderstanding. That my mom is lost without him and despite doing her all to give me everything, she still loses herself to the bottle far more times than I care to admit. I get to forget that my grandparents grow older and one day I won't have them either.

Tonight I get to drink, have fun and get to see the boy I like without Cassie's torment weighing me down. Tonight is about me and no one else. Something she doesn't see, but I get.

I get to see Hugh without her and in a completely distinct element than she does. Surrounded by friends and alcohol. A combination I've been dying to see and know it's something she'll never be privy to because she's not allowed to go out at night. And although I know it makes me a shitty friend, I can't help it.

I guess the saying is true, there is no helping who you fall in love with.

Because right about now, I wish I could fall out of love with the snap of my fingers. Although I don't get how she came to date him or what he saw in her. He's Jenine's brother and there's no love between her and Cassie.

My best friend hates the populars. Meanwhile, I want to be like them so I can have him. I'm a party animal. Wild, crazy, and funny. Hugh and I are practically a perfect match, yet he's dating my best friend.

Tangled and complicated like my entire life. What I feel for him is new and unexpected for me; love. But she took him away before I could shoot my chance with him. I'm really looking forward to seeing him tonight and perhaps getting the opportunity to talk to him in my own element.

I run my hand over my outfit one last time before walking up the steps to Jenine's house, already packed despite it still being a little early. But then again, not much of a surprise with it being a populars' party and everyone wanting to be in their good graces. Including me.

I waste no time finding myself a drink as the crowd begins to grow by the minute. Calm fills me with the feel of the place. I've been to plenty of parties, but none of them have been quite like this. Jenine's party feels just a little bit different from the ones I've been to.

A smile spreads across my lips as I look at the bustling horde of people and the loud music that has me dancing along to the rhythm. Letting loose on the dance floor sets me free, but by the fourth song, my throat is parched and I walk away in the search of a second drink. Weaving through the multitude proves to be a far more time-consuming task than expected, but it leads me to find the hosts of the party at the bar as I walk up to it.

Glee and fluttering butterflies run my nerves rampant as I find them both with half-full cups of the fruity alcoholic drink I drank earlier. A delicious one that I currently need and plan to drink down like water for the entire night. Without a second thought about the hangover, I'm certain I'll have tomorrow.

"Becca, I'm so glad you could make it," Jenine greets me as I get a hold of the drink I crave. "Loving the outfit, so populistic," she adds with a smile that I happily mirror, as I appreciate the outfit my best friend chose and bought for me.

Cassie has always had great taste. The strapless new lace top with a sweetheart neckline and the short turquoise skirt that stops just above my mid-thigh, paired perfectly with the synthetic black leather jacket and nude heels I had in my closet, just prove it. Not to mention the cute, small, nude handbag she had bought me was a nice touch.

"Thank you, Cassie..."

"Hugh, doesn't Becky look nice?" Jenine cuts me off as she nudges her brother, prying him for an answer to a question I was not expecting her to ask him.

"Very," he replies with a smile that has me blushing from

head to toe and my extremities tingling. I desperately pray that he writes it off as me having just come off the dance floor and not him noticing my infatuation for him.

"I have to go make sure the football players aren't wrecking my home in their fun, but I leave you in the best of company," she communicates to me with a grin and I nod in understanding. "Hugh, keep my guest of honor company. I wouldn't want her to have a terrible time at her first party," Jenine says sweetly to her brother before walking away from us, but my eyes remain transfixed on his to notice where she goes.

"My sister is right, you look amazing," he speaks the moment she's gone, his eyes surveying me up and down and I play with my curls to appear unaffected.

"Cassie chose my outfit," I confess and inwardly curse myself for bringing her up now, of all times. He nods slowly in thought as he takes another sip out of his cup and I fear having ruined it all as guilt churns in my stomach.

I down the rest of my drink in one go and take hold of another one. Hugh takes out a blunt and lights it up before bringing it up to his lips. I watch him take a drag and blow out the smoke in a relieved state. I breathe it in as he offers it up to me and I don't question it as I take the blunt and bring it up to my lips.

Our gazes remained locked as I take a hit, feeling the earthy smoke taste on my tongue that I can easily grow addicted to before releasing the breath of white smoke his way. A smirk lights up his features as I offer it back to him. His fingers brush a tad longer around mine as he takes it and my eyes close of their own volition as my body relaxes and my mind blanks.

There is just a beauty about smoking weed that Cassie will never understand and why I'll never tell her about it. It's calm and peaceful. A state of blankness where no worries exist. The world simply fades and the high is as if you were on a cloud. Something Hugh clearly gets.

We spend the rest of the night drinking, smoking, and dancing. Talking just about everything except Cassie and it's a breath of fresh air. Our bodies mold perfectly as we move to the beat of the music and the moment our lips meet, it feels as if I were in heaven.

I get lost in his touches and lips; living my best life. Foregoing leaving at three in the morning, as planned, when he leads me back towards his bedroom. The populars' parties are certainly the best and they aren't half bad. They resemble me and I'm certain most, if not all, of them have had sex with at least one guest tonight, but that's why these parties are so fun.

Hugh and I continue our personal party upstairs, even dancing to a slow song despite neither of us being able to stand properly and tumbling onto one another. Our words slur and our hands wander, but the moment our lips meet, I know it's game over. The liquor burns through my veins as we fall onto the bed and I give in to my feelings for him.

Letting him be my first. Gifting him my virginity and spending hours giving into our desires before falling asleep in each other's arms as the sun rays seep into the room.

A smile on my face as sleep takes a hold of me while thinking about this party being the best thing to happen to me. I gave my virginity to the guy I loved, and he made my dreams come true, but my best friend can never know about this.

She can't know he and I slept together. I love her too much to hurt her with the truth. My poor lapse in judgment tonight will be tomorrow's problem, along with the guilt I know will take a hold of me. But for now, I'll enjoy this.

Clearly, he feels something for me too or he would have never taken me to bed and now all that needs to happen is for them to break up. We can date like we were supposed to from the beginning. And I get to have them both without her getting hurt because I feel no guilt at the moment for being with him.

Hugh

I expected waking up with a hangover that could easily be my future cause of death. Doing so with Becca sleeping on top of me definitely wasn't. Regret and shock filled every aching fiber in my body as Cassie's face came to mind. I cheated on my girlfriend, but I don't feel a lick of regret.

A man has needs, and she never has to find out about this. Just like my buddies or I'll lose the game. They can't know I gave in to my attraction to Becca and slept with her before the end of the school year.

Maybe I could have held out more if Cassie actually put out, but despite my many attempts, her puritan ways won't break. If it weren't because I want to win the score on the pool, we have going on who can remain faithful the longest to nobodies like Cassie, then I would leave her.

Becca is clearly the better choice.

Dammit, I'm going to have to let my sister in on our little bets and finally cave into telling her my reason for being with Cassie. I hate letting her win, but I have no choice. I want to win, and I definitely can't give Becca up now that she's mine.

I'm certain I can convince her to keep it a secret and be my sidepiece just till the year ends.

Becca

Sleep begins to drift away at the feel of someone's gaze on me. A wonderful way to wake up since I know who it belongs to. Awareness to the events that transpired last night has my skin tingling as I open my eyes to look up at him. A smile that he mirrors with ease tugs at my lips.

It lessens my killer hangover in a second.

"Last night was amazing," I say with a grin at the want for this moment to last.

"I couldn't agree more, beautiful," he replies, sporting a full-blown smirk as his eyes rave my exposed flesh with clear want. So he wants a repeat of last night as much as I do, if his eyes are any sign.

I can get on board with that, but first, the elephant in the room has to be addressed because I cannot risk my best friend getting hurt.

"Hugh, Cassie can never find out about this," I blurt out in all seriousness. She can't know that I betrayed her for a boy and I can't ask either of them to leave the other one. I'm acutely aware that he offers her more time away from home and, more importantly, the monster in her bed.

I love her despite our differences. She's my best friend and I want to keep her safe and protect her the best way I can. That means taking a page out of her book, and being absolutely selfless no matter how much it may hurt.

She would either never understand my actions and, therefore, never forgive me. Or she'll leave him if I come clean to her about it all and we could work it all out. I'm betting on the latter happening but...

I won't risk her that way.

Knowing of the torment she goes through... I have to do everything I can to spare her more.

"I was about to tell you the same thing," he answers me with cryptic eyes. No doubt attempting to see why I beat him to the punch, but I will not reveal her secrets to anyone. We're each other's vaults. "But seeing as that is now settled, how about a repeat?"

The question gets lost as he flips us and hovers above me. I nod sheepishly, wrapping my arms around his neck. A smile crosses my lips before pulling his lips to mine and conveying with a kiss how much I love him, even if he'll never feel the same way.

I rather enjoy this, no matter how temporary it might be. As the saying goes, it's better to have lost and loved than not at all.

"Let's keep this just between us for now," he mutters against my lips, and it takes me a second to process his words. My words fail me, so I simply hum in agreement.

"Friends with benefits, then?" I breathe out the only thing it will ever be after managing to find my voice.

"Definitely," his lips find mine, sealing our agreement before getting lost in making love and foregoing both school and my best friend.

She can survive one day without me, I know it.

Just this one time.

I finally leave the Squire household close to two and head straight for the shower the moment I get home to scrub the night away, knowing there will be many more like them to come. Living in a bubble of joy as I change into a pair of shorts and an oversized t-shirt.

It lasts two hours before Cassie comes over and bursts it with her mere presence. Not that she will know, but I'm certain she notices something. We're best friends.

"You missed school today," she shoots straight to the point with eyes locked on mine the second my bedroom door is closed. "Why?"

Annoyance grows at those three words. Because of all the days, I need her to assume, today is the day I need her to. It would save me from lying.

But it makes sense she wouldn't.

"Huge hangover."

I opt for half-truths because she knows me too well.

"I called earlier and your mom said you still weren't home. So where were you?"

Her words leave me shell-shocked. I wasn't expecting her to have already questioned my whereabouts. Why couldn't my mom keep quiet just this once?

"Slept it off at Jenine's house," I snap at her, already done with this interrogation. I can't let it slip that I slept with Hugh. I'm not ready to let him go and she needs him to be away from the monster. "Is there a problem with that?"

She flinches at my words as if they had been a physical blow, and regret consumes me. I forget the power words have on her and it kills me to have said them. But the moment I see it on her face, it almost has me spilling everything.

"Becks, I know you love to party but you can't miss school," she explains softly and my mood sours.

"Don't overreact," I wave her off to avoid her oncoming lecture. I'm in no mood to hear it, less today of all days.

"You've already missed thirty-five days this year. I simply want you to pass and graduate on time," she beckons and guilt churns inside me. Why does she have to be so sweet and caring?

So unbelievably selfless...

"Oh, calm down, Miss Perfect," I snarl at her, far angry at myself than her. But also hate the feeling of being changed. Not everyone can get prime grades and has aspirations to go to college to be a vet like her.

"You know—"

"I know what I'm doing and have no plans to go to college. So save it," I cut her off with the truth. I don't know what I want to be, but know I'm not her, and never could be.

Frankly, right now I could do without her being the perfect friend right now because then I'll tell her everything about Hugh, and I can't do that. I love him, but she needs him. I don't want to feel bad for my actions.

"But—"

"Drop it," I warn her and she sighs.

"Fine, so how did the party go?"

Oh, God! What am I meant to tell her? I can't very well tell her I had sex with her boyfriend.

Popular

♥

Cassie

THREE MONTHS PASSED IN the blink of an eye since Becca went to that stupid party and it kills me to feel the void only growing. The only details I heard of the night were that it was an amazing party and that she gave her virginity away to some guy but refused to say more than that. Nothing more.

Well, no more truths, that is. Everything else was a lie. I just knew it deep down.

And I hate what it has done to us. For one, she spends far more time with the populars than me, but still, we remain best friends. Yet it feels like I'm losing her as the days pass by. I hardly recognize her.

We barely see each other because she's constantly partying with them and the few times that she's not, she spends the time talking about them. I'm forced to sit and nod at her words because the moment I tell her something about them, she'll snap. At times, even walk away.

It seems she's placed them on some stupid pedestal, which I can't get them off. She seems to think they're perfect little saints. Which wouldn't be a problem if they were, but they're not. She's simply blinding herself to the reality of the truth.

They're monsters, just like my stepfather. Simply a different breed. Witches like my stepmother.

Vile snakes that resort to violence, insults, and degradation against innocents for the sole pleasure of it.

"Cassandra, I thought I told you to clean the kitchen," Susan Pearce, my father's fourth wife, snaps at me. Her hand strikes me from behind before her bony fingers dig into my arm as she flings me off the couch and towards the one room, she needs pristine for her friends.

I fall to my knees at her brute force and hold back the tears already burning my retinas in an attempt to stay strong. How I hate this woman.

A conniving woman who loves and dotes on me in public, but the second we're out of view will throw every insult and blow she can to hurt me. Today is no different, since my dad is at the office doing who knows what.

For not the first time, I envy my father's other children with his other wives for not having to deal with this witch. I hate that I do but who would believe my word over the one of a saint? Even my mom sees her as nothing more than sweet.

If only she knew the truth. The things that this woman has uttered behind her back have left me broken on my mother's behalf. But just like with the monster at home, I'm bound to silence on her cruelties.

"Get to cleaning it now or you can forget about dinner," she threatens and I dip my head in acknowledgment as I wait for her to leave, choosing to remain silent.

It's not till I hear the clicking of her heels against the marble floors that I let the tears cascade down my cheeks. But I don't let it last more than a minute, knowing well my timetable and the truth of her words. If only Becca and I weren't currently so distant, I could call on her to come to save me, but everything has changed.

Instincts don't lie, people do. Right now, my best friend has other priorities and I can't talk to her as I once could, but I refuse to tell her. The image of her being so carefree with me but so somber with me weighs heavy in my memories.

I rather let the conversations revolve around her and seeing her smile. I truly don't mind except because it feels as if I'm competing with Jenine for her time. Where I could once say I would forever win, have been on the path of loss as of late. Nevertheless, I wish we were still as close as before Hugh came into the picture.

And the one positive thing that came from that stupid party is they now get along. They've even become friends, just like I wanted. But it couldn't have come at a worse time. Because despite things going pretty well, I simply harbor no more feelings for him.

Before I could overlook his social status in school, but now that my gut tells me he's hiding something; I can't. For someone who picks up on lies quickly, it's bothersome to be with a liar, but I don't know how to leave him. He still offers time away from my monsters.

Funny how they get along now that I could not care less about it. I even suspect that they're closer these days than she and I are. Something I hate admitting that I'm jealous about. They hang out far more, having the same circle of friends that don't involve me.

The times all three of us have hung out as of late have felt as if I've been the third wheel, but I wanted this so I can't complain. I asked them to get along.

Breathing in deeply, my hands work through the task at hand. Leaving the kitchen spotless and in perfect condition for my witch of my stepmother to host her gathering with her friends. For which I'm certain she'll take the credit.

If anything, I should hurry to finish before she has me cook instead of ordering out as she has planned. I have to get back to studying with school ending in a few weeks and final exams being right around the corner.

People truly don't know how much I struggle to keep up with assignments outside of school, but I'll write that off to them being blind and dead. I've screamed at the top of my lungs before and they've only filled with more water at each shout. Silent screams may not be heard, but the pain remains in my eyes.

The bruises that can be caught in glimpses. Tears during the day while a blanket is wrapped around my shoulders in comfort. The silence speaks for more than anything.

But they all ignore it. Everyone. They refuse to see the truth because it inconveniences them and I don't want to say it out loud only to be thrown into the deep end and called a liar.

Rather, the hell I know, then to make it worse.

Studying is my way out. I'll take every advanced course I can, look at college brochures, choose one, apply for scholarships, and then disappear the second I graduate. I'll leave them all to be happy and start anew.

I simply have to survive till then. A few years is nothing. I can do this.

Applying and being accepted in art college courses for the summer in New York and California is the first step. Something to keep me away from home and a possibility thanks to my dad being able to fulfill the costs they'll generate.

Plans are made. I just have to survive till they come to fruition.

Surviving the monster in my room and the witch of a wife my father has... it's never been harder, but as long as I keep my head down and stick to the silence, then it should work out. At least till summer, then I'll have a safe place with hundreds of miles between them and me.

Hell is hell, but I hardly remember a time when I haven't been in it, so it makes coasting through so much doable. Becks made it easier, but I need to quit drowning her with me. Best friends don't do that to one another.

And I am very much looking forward to her and I sharing a sixteen-birthday party in the upcoming weeks too. Parties mean little to me anymore, but they do to her, and sharing something like this with her means everything. It feels like old times. It'll be like them. I just know it.

Maybe I'll even be able to talk to Becks about joining me in visiting colleges soon. We could get an apartment together, I in school and she doing whatever she chooses to do that I'll wholeheartedly support. Hopefully, it's college too, but I don't plan to hold my breath or push her towards it.

I know I want to be a veterinarian because animals can't be as cruel as humans. But also, be going to art school at the same time because I enjoy doing multiple things. I know it'll be hard to balance both, but I have utter faith that I can do so. It'll keep me busy and definitely won't be able to come home.

And by the time I'm done with both, I won't have to.

I may not have been able to do it all in the future, but I know I will do two things that truly make me happy. Not to mention if one fails, I'll have a backup plan; a contingency plan to save me.

That's more than smart.

After all, my only dream is to get away from here.

Becca

Popularity was far more than I ever expected it to be. It was beyond intoxicating and it's easy enough for me to recognize why Jenine loves it so much. I love it so damn much that I'm uncertain if I'll ever be able to give it up.

Which is pure nonsense because I won't ever have to. Jenine and I have grown close and in a short time, she's become a great friend. Nowhere near Cassie. Despite that, I see the potential for it to be more. For her to be another person I can call best friend and that thought makes me smile more times than not.

To have a friend who actually gets me is everything. One who shares my same interests and has no desire to change me is quite refreshing. A true relief I wish I'd only gotten sooner.

"Beautiful, what are you thinking about?" Hugh's voice breaks through my mindless thoughts and its absolute glee to be normal and free of the heavyweights of trauma.

And Hugh is as normal as there could be. He and Jenine are it. Not to mention the ribbons of popularity adorning them are beyond fucking great.

"Nothing," I reply to his question, to which he quirks an eyebrow in response.

"How can nothing make you smile?"

"Because it's normal," I quip, but he continues to harbor the same puzzled look that shows I need to change the subject. He doesn't get the meaning of pain, unlike Cassie or me. My mother is resembling more of an alcoholic this day and my father is dead.

None of that mentioning that my grandparents' medical bills are piling up and have led to more strains than not in my family. Everyone has an opinion on everything but not wanting to actually be there or see the effects of their choices. Typical.

Something only Cassie got. But I choose to push her aside because of the guilt growing in my stomach every day; especially when I see the hidden bruises and winces. The moment my eyes meet her hollow ones, I'm instantly filled with regret every single time.

But my coping mechanism involves letting loose. Going out to parties, smoking, and drinking despite the hangover I know I'll have the next day. It's a vicious cycle, but sharing it with Hugh makes it far too addicting to ever consider leaving.

"So, tell me, big boy, do we have the house to ourselves or..."

The opening and closing of the front door answers my question, and I smile at the thought of seeing Jenine. I cuddle more into Hugh's chest, but he pushes me off and places distance between us almost immediately, which alarms me.

Does he want to end what we have?

So soon?

My brain spirals into a wormhole of what-ifs as a couple joins us in the living room. I look at them confused and bounce my gaze between them and Hugh, only for it to dawn on me. They're his parents.

The ones that Jenine has made a note to say are always traveling. Surely, she would know they were coming home... Here he and I are utterly alone in their home while he has a girlfriend, who is my best friend. Not my best moment and I should probably leave.

"Mom, dad! Jeni, know you're home?" Hugh questions them both after greeting them with a hug that they affectionately return.

"Why should she?" His mother questions him with a sweet tone, but the way she brushes Jenine off rubs on me all the wrong way. The woman looks affectionate and gentle, but having been around Cassie and her monsters, I know better than to fall for appearances.

"Right," I mutter under my breath as I rise from the couch. "Well, I have to head out, so I'll see you later." The truth flows with ease out of my lips and I thank my lucky stars for having an excuse to escape these people.

My insides churn at their sight and the way they disregarded their daughter. I have enough experience with the stepwitch to recognize her kind. And right now, I have to rescue Cassie from her claws.

"I hope you're not leaving on our behalf," his father swoops in with a kind smile that pricks my skin with unease. It seems so familiar but I'm unable to place it and instead choose to brush it aside. No sense in analyzing it when I'm leaving.

"I have plans with my best friend," I answer with a smile and a shrug. "And I'm sure you want to spend time alone with your son, without his friend meddling," I add to transition my escape. I know these excuses by heart now.

Nostalgia hits me at the thought of excuses. Cassie always

did call me the queen of them and remembering us sitting on my bedroom floor while we crafted every pretext possible to escape hell... makes my heart hurt. Both by my betrayal and the void that has grown between us.

Maybe a sleepover is in order. Hugh can survive without me for a few nights.

"Well, it was nice meeting you," I add, before making a beeline for the front door. Not even bothering to wait for an answer as an immense need to see Cassie overwhelms me. Her father's house is only a few blocks from here, so there is no need to text anyone to pick me up and give me a lift.

I have every intention of walking, but somewhere along the way, the urge simply grows and my legs end up picking the pace. Going from walking to fast-walking, to jogging till I run. Stopping to catch my breath only when I'm outside their impressive two-story brick house her father lives in.

The second my lungs get a good mouthful of oxygen; my feet race to the door and my knuckles hit against the door. My eyes catch sight of the doorbell a minute later and I'm pressing it twice both because I know it annoys the woman and I don't need her pretending she heard nothing.

It takes three minutes for the door to open to reveal the blond in question with a genuine smile on her face. One that morphs into a fake one the second her eyes find me. No doubt she was waiting for someone else.

And not for the first time; I come to wonder if she has a lover on the side and is simply with Cassie's dad for his cash. The man is well off for sure. I know the houses in this area are at the very over half a million dollars at the very least, so the idea is plausible.

"Becca, I didn't know you were stopping by," she says with a sly tone that alerts me to gouging of information. Which means I did the right thing by coming. Bitch probably has Cassie doing absurd chores that she can pay someone for. I only pray that she hasn't raised her hand against her. "Cassie didn't mention anything."

A smile mirroring her fake one plasters on my lips at her words. Had Cassie told her, she would have found a way for pretenses or she simply wouldn't have listened. This woman knows the power I have in knowledge and what it can cost her if I were to speak.

She just doesn't know I would never put my friend in the position of being robbed of her own story. I wouldn't expose her truths without her wanting to. She's my vault as much as I am hers.

"I figured I would surprise her and seeing as exams are coming..."

"Right, Cassie is a brainiac after all," her tone drops an octave as if she were mocking my best friend, but knowing her, she probably is.

"You know it," I quip.

"She's in her room. I imagine you know where it is by now," she points out and although I want to inconvenience her by saying no and having her take me, I don't. I care more about getting rid of her right now.

So, I nod, and as she steps to the side; I make my way through the house toward the back, where Cassie's room is. I don't bother with knocking and simply enter, only to find her looking at herself in the mirror.

My heart stops as I see new bruises on her arm and my instincts have me wanting to rip that woman downstairs to shreds. Both of her stepparents are utter horror. How her parents can be with them...

It takes her a minute to see me, but the second she does, she pulls the sleeves down and swivels on her feet. She gives me a genuine smile that just breaks my soul because, as always, despite the pain, she rather not worry anyone.

"I was thinking of you earlier. Did you read my mind?"

"Like best friends do. You know I had to come and save you from the step witch," I joke and humor reflects in her eyes. "How about a sleepover?"

"Like old times?" She questions and I dip my head in

agreement. "I would love to, feels like we haven't had one in forever."

Guilt hits me again. I've been leaving her to fend for her own... Pushing her to the side for Jenine and popularity. I've been selfish and need to do better. As I look into her hopeful eyes, I vow to do so.

"It does, but promise you I'll do better about it. At least one sleepover a week."

"And your parties?"

"I don't have to go to every single one, and if anything, it'll make me more popular to not go to every single one," I quip, and the smile she gives me is everything.

My heart still won't let me go of Hugh yet, but maybe it's time to actually start trying because betraying her hurts. I can come clean and we can both leave him. We only have two more years of school, anyway.

Anything for her. Cassandra Castillo is the best of best friends and I will do right by her once again.

Summer

Cassie

SUMMER COMES IN THE blink of an eye. One second I'm killing myself studying for my finals and the very next, school is out. Becks and I having a sleepover a week with the promise to have more like before, but her status as a popular now always get in the way.

So I quit holding my breath at her promises for more. Instead, I enjoy the ones we do have because something is better than nothing with her. Especially when our conjoined birthday party gets ruined as she bails on me last moment for some extravagant one Jenine throws for her last minute.

Same day as ours. Where I wasn't even invited; warned by Jenine not to go and by Becca not to. So, I canceled everything on ours as parties no longer mean anything to me. I only ever did look forward to it because of her.

And why put myself through the joy of a party only to have it stolen later on by the monster when he gives me his 'very special gift' when my bedroom door closes? Why even fight it when I know nothing is going to change?

No one likes the screams of a victim, anyway. It inconveniences them. I'm an inconvenience.

It hurt to be cast aside once more for my bully, but I let it be. Becks smiles and is normal by her side, so it's okay. She's allowed to have other friends. Even if they aren't mine.

Our birthday was hell for me, but heaven for her. So small mercies and all.

The next day was full of packing, as I would leave for my internship in New York the day after that. So, I spent it double-checking everything and was happy till the moment that man came in and claimed what he always did from me.

My soul was far too battered, knowing full well the cost by now, to have fight-or-flight instincts. The knowledge and extent that the bruises would have on me kept my tears silent and my screams internal. I rather not have to excuse them with lies for my parents.

The monster held that power over me. As did the step-witch. By now, they both knew that I would keep quiet to spare others from pain. Dad loves her. Mom, him. And my siblings...

Although my mind sometimes would contemplate the thought of them getting together; deep down I knew it would never happen. There would be no one to pay for the broken plates. Still, it played as a fantasy.

The pain they each inflicted on me was different, but they all enjoyed breaking me. They thrived on my tears; my destruction and being broken. Susan, Luis, and Jenine were all the same.

Becca always encouraged me to fight against the stepwitch and the monster. She always spoke about breaking the silence, but how can I tell her I lost the feeling of self-preservation? Abuse is tricky that way, I suppose.

You lose who you are along the way... But once I go to college, I'll find myself and finally heal. Till then, I have to keep holding on.

Nowadays, she forgets most things, but not everything is about me. I know that and it's nice to hear things that bring her glee. Even if it involves my tormentor at school. The wolf in sheep's clothing she no longer sees.

I let her be free from my hell. It's mine to live and endure.

If she no longer wants to indulge in conversations about it, then I have to respect her choice. It has to mean that it doesn't have any meaning, and she has faith in me to survive on my own.

And Becks would never lie to me.

That thought made me smile the next morning as I left for New York before the sun ever rose into the sky. Not that I ever went to sleep that night. It was nice to have a reprieve from the monster at home as I had my dad drive me to the airport.

Spending time simply the two of us was everything, as his wife never rose before ten. The talks we would have renewed my hope that one day I wouldn't be broken and we could all be happy even if apart. Because it's clear to me that to be happy, I have to be away from my monsters and that includes leaving my family, too.

But it'll be okay because they will be happy.

It will be for the best, even if it hurts.

They'll see that one day, I know it.

"It's time," dad states as we finish checking in my bags and I nod with a small smile, holding on tight to my purse. My short escape is a bittersweet moment for us both, but far more for me than for him.

"It is," I say a quick second later.

"Are you sure you're up for this?" He questions, turning to face me and I dip my head as an answer.

"I am. I'm really excited," my voice comes out strong and certain. The closest it has been to a normal teenager. I'll be away from the monster who does unholy things to me when there aren't eyes on us. Away from the woman who berates me with words as much with her hands.

I'm able to let loose and be myself. Free of fear. With no one to hurt me in the shadows.

The best thing to happen to me in a long time.

"Call every day," he voices, and I wrap my arms around him.

"I promise," I whisper before pulling away. A temporary goodbye that'll bring me nothing but glee. Becks would be proud.

I know she already is.

Smiling, I give him one last embrace before walking away without turning back to pass through airport security. The whole process taking but forty minutes, leaving me enough time to spare to get something at a restaurant before having to board the plane.

I'll nap on the airplane.

Or so was the plan, but the sights from the clouds mesmerized me. My problems all lifted and stayed behind. Landing in New York was a true breath to my aching lungs that would forever remain with me.

With no one to fear, I could hide between people and enjoy the course, which was truly amazing. Spending my free time taking photos and doing tourism around the city. Doing everything with a genuine smile on my lips. Calling my parents and Becca every single day as she spent her summer with Jenine and the populars.

Made temporary friends and got a taste of how life would be once I left home and went to college. It was bliss and passed far too fast. My grin fell the moment I had to go home and the thought of staying in New York forever crossed my mind.

But the questions stopped me. What would I do? Where would I go? I knew no one here and my parents didn't deserve that. At least with college, they would get some sort of heads-up.

So, I packed with a haunted heart, knowing what awaited me at home. Abuse and pain. Being the punching bag for the witch and monster. I sobbed the entire night about what was to come. Cried silent tears on the plane.

Washing it away with cold water splashed on my face and lied about it being jet lag. A lie that was believed far too easily for my liking. My lungs were heavy when my mother and *him* met me at the airport. Despair and anxiety ate at me the entire way home.

Bid my time by sketching to keep myself from drowning in hell. Because four weeks in New York were nothing. As the saying goes; 'When you're happy, time flies by.'

Even seeing my father and siblings couldn't brighten my mood. They stayed afloat because I drowned for them every single day. Not that they'll never know. I can never be the root of their pain.

So, I smiled through it all.

Keeping in mind that I would only be here for a week and then I would travel to California. Pretending is what I do best now, anyway. Becks wasn't there, as she returned from her vacation after me.

I got to see her and Hugh twice that week. Once the day they came back and then spend time with each of them one on one. Time with her was just like old times, but with him... it was uncomfortable.

We hung out two days before I went to California with him talking about sex and me telling him no. He persisted until I caved, not really wanting to. It didn't feel right, but he wanted to and I wanted him to shut up.

But nothing happened as his sister interrupted us before anything could really happen. It was nothing more than a heavy make-out session. I left questioning why I let it even get that far, to begin with; wondering if it was because the monster stole my virginity a long time ago and I know nothing else.

Regret filled me, but going to California would help clear my mind. I left with thoughts of breaking up with him while smiling on the plane. Certain that time apart would give me the clarity I needed.

Pushing him out of mind and doing exactly what I did in New York. Sightseeing, taking photos, enjoying myself, and letting myself be free. No monster or witch for weeks to come. Four weeks without being broken.

It was the happiest I'd ever been. Treasured moments I would carry forever. Enjoying the sun and indulging in trips to the beach. With the art course being impeccable once more. Expanding my skills and artistic eye.

Yet, just like in New York, time passed far too quickly. During those trips, I did something that I'd never done before: be selfish. Something that I can't be back home and I missed the feeling the second I set foot in the airport as it evaporated like droplets of water in the blazing sun.

California was simply me time. Where my contact back home was limited to texts. Not thinking even once of Hugh. Becks was occasionally in my thoughts, but those were more limited to us living together in a brand-new city.

Texts with them both were flitting, but through my glee, it slipped past me as if it were nothing. Most of my responses comprising single-worded texts as they complained about the exhaustion that accompanies popularity. Neither once questioned how things were going with me, and I kept from bringing it up after being called self-centered when speaking of my day.

Yet, as always, the chains of selflessness gripped tight to my flesh as I landed once more in Dallas, Texas, two days before school began. The second Hugh heard I was home, he came to see me and took me out on a date. He was sweet and caring once more; nothing like when I was away.

When he brought sex away, I felt powerless to say no. He was nice and... we were dating. Hearing his reasons only added to my guilt of being broken and I caved, barely reacting to his touch. It felt like when the monster stole my voice away from prying eyes and I was left far more confused after.

But at least this time it was by choice, right?

It still didn't stop me from feeling filthy and scrubbing at my skin in the shower. Two months away had given me the clarity that I sought; left it clear that I simply wanted to focus on myself and my education. College is my only way out and I want to leave. I know that.

I can't afford distractions. Hugh is a huge one, but dating is unknown to me despite us being together. How do people break up?

And maybe a minor part of me didn't want to because he keeps me away from home. In some small way Hugh protects me from the monster grappling my body when no one is looking and I want him away whatever means it takes. Is it so bad to use Hugh for a little while longer?

Maybe it is possible to focus on me and my education while he stays around. Letting him take me out sometimes. God has to be on my side once, right?

Reason why when school started back up, I began taking as many college courses as possible. I need to have as much of a head start as is possible. More homework, but not impossible. Becks hangs out more with Jenine and her posse anyway, so I have no reason to worry about her.

She hardly answers my calls or messages since summer break and we hardly spend any time together anymore. I can't deny that it hurts, but I have to respect her and focus on surviving. She knows I'm here for her.

And I'm not standing in the way of her dream, no matter how much I hate it. She deserves to be happy.

Even if her avoidance is a clear sign that she's hiding something from me. But none of that takes away from the fact she's like a sister to me. Far more than my own because she knows it all. Though despite that, it's beginning to feel that she's no longer the person I used to know.

Less my best friend and more like my tormentors. Popularity is clearly a vile disease. Makes me wonder if it rotted all the monsters in my life.

Jenine has it. No doubt Susan has it. And Luis? He would never hurt a fly; let alone abuse his stepdaughter.

And now Becca, my best friend, gets off on bullying other kids to fit in. I never knew she could be so cruel, and if it weren't for our entire history and she being the only one I had; I would have probably already given up on her.

Which leaves our friendship in thin air. Fragile like glass. Something I desperately wish I could fix, but I can't. Not alone anyway.

She needs to be willing, as I am, and she isn't. Only my best friend could repair it; not the fake lecherous person who has replaced her. Because it may look like her, but it isn't. My best friend knew pain and wouldn't inflict it on others so willingly. Not to mention she actually cared about me and never sought me only when she needed something.

The means to which our friendship has now been reduced to. But I still give it to her. Deep down, my heart harbors the hope that it's all salvageable. That I haven't lost the one thing God had allowed me to keep.

A being I'm not beginning to doubt because he's never there when I need him, despite praying to him every night. He's not there when I cry myself to sleep. He's not there when I ask for comfort and strength in the church. Nor in the priests I've gone to, to help me heal.

As much as my mom talks about him and says praying helps keep all the nightmares away. He has yet to have shown up for me or help me at all. None of it helps, and I'm even questioning why I let my mom drag me to church to sit there and talk about a benevolent, all-powerful being who has never manifested for me.

If he were to exist, then he's nothing of the sort. Because who could be okay with what happens to me? I've heard so many stories of people saying he saved them, but never me. Clearly, I'm the problem.

Because I know something has happened between Becca and me, and I can't even get her to tell me. My soul knows Jenine is only using her to destroy me, but despite me telling her repeatedly my suspicions; she won't listen. She thinks I'm jealous of her popularity.

We argue now more than ever and she now harbors secrets from me.

She's far closer to Hugh these days. My boyfriend who has

also changed. Back to being distant and colder than he's ever been. Side effect of finally giving him what he wanted; sex. Now it's all he wants and I find myself unable to tell him no because, clearly, I no longer have any self-preservation in me left.

Funny how the dream was to wait till marriage, yet my innocence was robbed by a monster and I handed myself so easily to my first boyfriend. My resolution not as strong as I had thought.

Clear hate for that three-letter word has rooted deep inside me, but I don't want to be back home full-time.

Life is just becoming more difficult by the day and I'm honestly growing tired of it all. I don't know anymore how long I can last underwater while everyone keeps afloat. They may not know it's at my cost, but they're pretty good at writing me off.

Secrets

Jenine

THINGS ARE ALIGNING TO perfection. My plans forming and coming to fruition with simple nudging. My brother proved to have been far more useful than I ever expected him to be.

God works in mysterious ways and it shows he has a weak spot for me. He should, seeing he should have given me parents like Cassandra Castillo. Giving her four parents who are actually in her life. Susan Pearce being one of them.

I've met the woman. She's fashionable, charitable, and the mother... I want.

Just like Gilbert McCormick is the father I would want. One to drive me to school and take me shopping when I want. I've seen them and it pisses me off.

But slowly I will take it all away from her. I'm already getting Becky, who, as predicted, is the perfect friend and accomplice.

The one I deserve. Someone actually on my level. If only her family would quit talking about Cassie and take a liking to me.

After all, I help pay their medical bills to win their favor. Ungrateful people, really. If it weren't because I can't truly win Becca without them, then I would have already sent them to hell.

But they're a means to an end. Only for that, I can hold on. Money buys everything. My father has shown me that well.

While my mother has taught me, looking impeccable is a must. It'll show them who the true queen of the hive is. There can only be one.

Me.

Looking flawless. A diet based on water and an apple a day. Unless I indulge in a salad or some other food, then its fingers shoved as deep into my mouth as they'll go to rid myself of the potential of extra pounds.

Beauty is pain. People don't crave ordinary, they want perfect. I'll do everything to be perfect. Popularity is perfection.

By default, I'm quintessential.

Soon the world will be molded into what I want as it should have been. They'll all answer to me and I'll swat the bees that serve me no purpose. It's give in to facts, or be destroyed.

No, in-between.

The school will get that. Students will get that. They'll all want to be, and I'll be immortal.

"Jeni," Fanilea's voice reminds me I'm not alone to be lost in thought. Only a fool wanting to lose their place would be arrogant enough to zone out. Especially before their rule is set in stone. Mine is close, but not there yet.

It will be the second Cassandra Castillo is destroyed. I have plans to turn everyone against her to have them show me their loyalty. A recognition of who the queen bee at this school is. The ultimate success.

My parents will have to give me their attention then. I'll be living up to the Squire name once and for all. If need be, I'll even make Craig my king, or personal jester, because I'm not sharing my title with anyone. He can be on his knees for me.

"Jenine," I remind her as she continues to file my nails.

"You let Becca call you Jeni."

"Because Becky is different," I snap at her as she sets the nail file to apply nail polish to my pristine nails.

"Right," she agrees without a fight. Perfect little minion. That's why I utterly love her. Will follow me without question.

"You had something to say?"

"I saw Grazella today with another girl," she answers my question and icicles stab at my heart. The unhealed wound of our broken relationship having it bleed all over again.

The girl has no taste or anything remotely interesting, and yet she wormed her insignificant way into my heart. Sad how she had to be cut loose and never could understand we were never to be more. Bringing her to my parents would have gotten me to lose the progress I have.

Craig might be an utter airhead, but he has something between his legs that she doesn't. That one thing is crucial for my parents' approval of me. I don't undergo all these trials for anything.

Thankfully, my current toy gets that. She's simply happy with my attention, as it should be. That is more than enough.

Still, it hurts to hear the girl I love despite her being nothing is dating someone new. How I wish she hadn't moved schools so I could keep them all away from her. She would have crawled her way back to me at some point. I know it.

"So?" I question Fanilea, uninterested yet wanting every bit of information she had. I will not arm my enemies with information, and they are all enemies.

"She's dating that girl you don't like," she adds.

"What girl?"

I don't like many. Her words are meaningless unless she elaborates.

"That junior that tried to—"

"You don't possibly mean whom I think you mean..."

"I saw them kissing," she goes on and rage overwhelms me. Oh, I'm ruining nobody's lives now. Screw the waiting game. I need the information to destroy Cassandra Castillo now to appease my broken heart now. Her tears will make do.

I've been far too comfortable in this running to get them

all at my beck and call. Time to up my game and get the details I need out of Becky before I go do something stupid like confess to my ex and beg for her to take me back. I will not send all my efforts to hell.

She isn't worth it. My heart needs to settle on a guy for my parents to love me. Others have the luxury of choosing, I don't. Not if I want to win and Jenine Squire always wins.

Becca

A year, six months, and three weeks since Hugh and I became lovers. Close to nineteen months since we began to see each other on the daily behind Cassie's back. Meeting nearly every day to give in to our desires despite how wrong it might be.

Guilt doesn't eat at me as it once did, and it scares me. It feels like I'm changing, but I've never been one to be easily manipulated. Still it...

Things are different. Very different.

For one, Jeni and I are far closer than Cassandra and I are. Hugh and my best friend slept with each other; to which I rejected him for three days straight the second I found out. But like always, he held my heart and sweet-talked me back into bed.

I hate admitting that I was far more afraid he would end things between us than I was being angry at him. She's too sweet and innocent for him. She deserves better, and he already had me. So why sweet talk her into the same promiscuous activities we take up with one another?

But that fear disappeared when he came to me and begged me. I suppose Cassie wasn't good enough for him. He admitted as much himself, bitching about how stiff she was during it all. My heart broke for her.

So much so, I snapped at him, left him alone, and went to her. He doesn't know her torment, but I do. No matter how close Jeni and I are, Cassie remains my best friend.

I care for her. Love her. How can I not? She's an absolute angel and our friendship goes all the way back since we were three years old. Something as pure as that doesn't simply break, but a huge part of me wants to give the title away and give it to Jeni.

After all, she and I are far more similar. Cassie doesn't know the meaning of fun and wants to change me. Get me to pay attention in school and eventually go to college. She seeks to turn me into her.

Not happening.

My best friend can be a doormat, and that is not me. That'll never be me. Being an angel is not for me.

She's the saint.

Unlike Jeni. Who understands me more than I've ever thought possible. Someone I can talk to without a filter.

We spend countless hours talking about it all. My mother slowly spiraling into an alcoholic. My grandparents' health declining and she helping cover costs. Even us talking about her parents rejecting her for being bisexual. Something I found out a little after my first party at her house when I found her with a girl.

She's gotten me to try new things. Such as playing together on her parents' yacht in the Maldives with Hugh and her little toy as well. A fun and exhilarating experience that led to me learning that I wasn't as straight as I thought.

It felt nice to have someone to talk to about it. A self-discovery that bound our friendship as she never judged me.

Our summer was one of the best ones I had. Going with them was everything and more. Hugh and I sharing a romantic getaway in the Caribbean while Cassie was in New York was liberating. Sun, parties, and a genuine relationship with Hugh. A memorable trip.

Meeting with the rest of our friends only to party as they

pushed us to date after finding out we were sleeping with one another. They were all very vocal in their desires for him to leave Cassie for me and it made me smile. Everyone knew how perfect we were for one another.

Jeni is the biggest voice on that front. But I can't help wondering if in her case it's because of the bad blood she and Cassie share. Still, it makes me happy to hear it and to have her approval. If she wants to destroy her; then that's her business. It might be the way to break away from Cassie, and I get to date Hugh.

I already avoid her like the plague because I can't face her. She is a vortex with endless pain, and I want the bliss of ignorance. I don't want to be sucked into it. Reason I ignore her attempts at communication.

But I don't want her death in my conscience, so I keep the sleepovers. She gets a break from hell and I'm helping. I've tried to do more, but what can I do? I've already scratched the man's car and told the witch her truths. Frankly, she could do more to get it to stop.

It's beginning to grate on me she doesn't.

Poor, helpless Cassie can't defend herself. Too gullible and innocent. Would rather break herself than her family. Far too selfless.

I don't know if it's noble or stupid, but I have to wonder nowadays if it's an act and she's come to enjoy it. No one holds a gun to her head. She would have told me I know it.

She's cried herself to bed for about fourteen years now and has even indulged in the idea of death once. But one call to me and she never went through with it. I talked her out of it and I'm happy I did.

It's how she came to admit everything to me. Her stepfather has truly hurt and broken her in every way possible and what little he hasn't, the stepwitch has taken care of. I simply hate that she'll never call it as it is.

Abuse. Rape. Bullying.

There is a difference between discipline and abuse, no

matter what people may see. Truth is, her witch of a stepmother beats her in places no one will see and use knives as words when she can't. The blows will never last long enough for Cassie to gain the courage and have proof.

End of the day, it's her word against Susan.

Meanwhile, her stepfather is sick and enjoys exploiting her for sexual pleasure. He should do so with her mother, not see his daughter as a woman. Daughter because for as long as he's been with Olivia, she's as much his daughter as she is Gilbert's.

She's helpless, or at the very least, that's how she paints it. But she should do more...

I can't keep being there for her. I want to live my life too. I want Hugh for myself, not to share him with her. But what choice do I have? He's only still with her because of me. But I'm growing tired.

Fatigued from hearing her talk about what goes on at home. Maybe she should check herself into a mental hospital to get away. They can help her heal, right?

Still, my family compares me to her because she's perfect in their eyes. I'm simply the disappointment who has to take care of herself and them. They don't quite like Jeni, and make it quite known. It's frustrating.

Cold hands cover my eyes from behind on my way to my next class. My heart races at the touch, wanting it to be Hugh and not some loser. I quite like the idea of being able to recognize him. But more than that, I don't want to lose him because someone wanted to be cute.

"Guess who?"

The question is all I need to know it's him. His voice is always a dead giveaway. But I would never admit it to him.

"Hmm... Hugh Squire," I tease with a hum.

"Correct, now for your prize," he answers, spinning me to face him and connecting our lips in an explosive kiss. His desire for me quickly becomes clear as the space between us disappears and my body heats at the thought. Doesn't matter that we're in the hallway full of other students who wouldn't dare tell Cassie.

Oxygen becomes very much needed for our lungs and we're forced to separate. I curse the air for being an essential piece of survival. He slips a note into my hand and pulls away. I smile as my hands unfold the piece of paper, but immediately halt at the sight of Cassie nearing us.

I sigh and hide it in my backpack before she can even see it.

"Hey you two," she greets us, and Hugh wraps an arm around her shoulders. She leans into him and jealousy fills me while her eyes remain glued to mine. To think if she hadn't interrupted us, we would currently be on our way to doing unholy things to one another.

I would be giving him pleasures she can't.

"Nothing," I reply with a tight smile. "So, are you sleeping over tonight?" I question and she smiles at me while her eyes show infinite relief.

"I am," she answers, and I nod. Hugh's eyes question me, but I shrug in response. Her secrets are her own. We're each other's vault. Her death will not be on my conscious.

The only guilt I feel is leaving her at home to party. This will make it go away.

"Brought your things with you, or do we have to stop to get them?" I ask, and her eyes morph into endless voids of pain. But in a second she hides it behind a smile. Hypocrite. Calling the populars the very thing she is.

She lies as much as the rest of humanity.

"Can you go with me to get them after school?"

The second the question is out, I know why. He's home. The pedophile abuser, who is one of the many reasons she cries at night, is home. Anger washes over me at the thought, but my brain needs confirmation.

"Sure, is *he* home?"

Her eyes drop and that's the only answer I need. Verbal confirmation be damned now. She knows it too, as she nods at me.

Once more, I'm overwhelmed with the need to protect her. He hurts her and I hate it. But once more, what can I do? What am I meant to do?

It should be her parents' problem. They should see the signs because they're there. But they don't.

Love is blind, something I know well if I analyze my relationship with Hugh. Once more regret churns at my insides. Here I'm sleeping with her boyfriend and being happy while she suffers. Being raped by that monster.

I used to keep her out of her house with sleepovers and spending time with her. But that's changed. I've made new friends. Moved on and left her behind.

I've achieved my goal, and it's bittersweet. I'm doubting her words yet am battling against my emotions. Helping her and wanting to ruin her. Trying to decide if she's truthful or a liar. It's a war inside me, but right now I simply want to strangle the man for hurting her.

Eyes of the Truth

Cassie

BECCA'S MOOD SOURED AT the mention of Luis being home. Her once smile was gone and her eyes reflected pure anger. Her hands balled into fists as if she wanted to beat someone up. I know who.

My stepfather. I don't need the words. Her reaction is enough. She knew how far he had broken me.

I didn't need to be explicit with my words. She could always read between the lines. She's known of the torment I've been living with since I was two years old from the man that took the role to help raise me when I was months old. I couldn't be more thankful that she has been there for me through it all.

I don't know what I would do without her. Probably be dead.

Becks knows far too much. How it began with words that led to neglect to bruises that faded far too quickly. Eventually, even escalating to rape; although the most I've told her is him getting on top of me, rubbing his body over mine. She knows.

I've spent my entire lifetime crying myself to bed because the pain is that great. For years I thought him to be my father, which made every act far more painful till I found out the truth when I was eleven. He wasn't.

At twelve, I sought and found my biological father. Established a relationship with him and made him a part of my life. I had thought it never would happen, but it did.

His wife never did like me, showing to be just like the monster but a different breed.

But I would be a liar if I said I sought Gilbert McCormick because my innocence was already stolen. No, before my dad came into my life, it was simply unwanted touches. The second he came in... it became rape.

Luis Anas no longer felt the need to hold himself to the standard of being my father. He no longer had to hold back on his evil. I drowned before I could even reach the surface for a breath of air.

I still remember the hurt mixed with feelings of guilt and shame. Words tried to part from me back then, but they never emerged afloat. I was warned into silence with a beating seen as discipline.

My dad stood up for me when he saw the bruises, but I was also shown no one would believe me. Drugs were bought and planted in my room. Everyone turned on me. Mom cried.

I lived with my dad for two months because of it. But I never told Becks that. I was afraid she would turn on me, too.

So, I kept to snippets but never told her the true extent of it all. I've always been too afraid to speak. But am I to be blamed? I was shown no one would believe me over something serious.

"Becky, you, okay?" Hugh questions her as she glares at the lockers. She's fuming, unable to calm down. My eyes pleaded with hers. "You look like you want to kill someone."

"I'm fine, simply thinking of someone I crossed paths with earlier," she spits, and I can read the lie. But I don't poke at it. That leads to questions that I can't answer or handle.

"What happened?" I ask playing the game. Rather, a lie that

hurts no one than a truth that breaks my entire family.

"Some girl called me a plastic Barbie and dared push me to the floor," she breathes through gritted teeth. My eyebrows furrow at the truth in her tone, but I also know it's not why she's currently angry.

"Tell Jeni so she can put the bitch in her place. Populars take care of their own," Hugh says in a bleeding, arrogant tone. The want to slap him hits me hard. But it quickly fades.

I could never resort to violence.

"I should," Becca replies, breathing out. Shock fills me.

She can't be serious? Jenine will make their life miserable; no one deserves that! Becks isn't like this, so why is she agreeing with him? Why is he even suggesting it? This is not the way. I have to make her see that.

"No, you shouldn't!" I voice scolding them both. I know by heart, violence leads nowhere. One only has to look at me to realize that. Broken and wishing for the day I graduate to leave home and never come back.

Becks can find a better way and maybe she needs to be reminded how terrible her new friend can be.

"Jenine destroys everything around her and no one deserves such a cruel punishment," I snap. "She's the plastic Barbie who uses everyone to her mere convenience!"

"Cassandra, that's my sister you're talking about," Hugh's voice elevates as if that'll frighten me. But he doesn't know I have no self-preservation instincts. They've all been stolen away. "She's none of the sort, and you don't know her."

He may be blind to Jenine's true nature, but I know the monster she truly is. Doesn't matter that she's his sister, it doesn't erase the truth. If anything, this boy is like her and I don't even know why I keep dating him.

"No, she is," I reiterate. "If you don't wish to admit it, then it isn't my problem, but yours. Everyone knows it, including her."

"Excuse you?" Becca questions me, offended and pissed. "How dare you speak to him like that? Hell, how dare you condemn Jeni when you know not a lick about her! You are such a damn hypocrite, Cassie, throwing stones at my best friend when your glass house would break if done to you."

I flinch at her words and the look of pure hatred in her eyes. I'm her best friend. Not Jenine. Me.

"I'm your best friend, not her," I correct her with hurt in my tone.

"You haven't been my best friend for a long time," Becks remarks with disgust. "She likes me for who I am, unlike you. She doesn't try to change me into a goody two shoes like you. If anything, the only reason I'm still your friend is that I feel sorry for your pathetic ass."

Her words stun me into silence. Tears burn my retinas. Frogs get lumped in my throat.

When did I lose my best friend to the girl that hates me because I was the teacher's favorite back in first grade? Mad that I got the seat she wanted. One who torments me over nothing?

When did Becca become like her?

"Get things straight, Cassandra; we're not the same. You're nothing but an idiot who believes far too highly of herself when she is clearly not," her insults are knives to my heart. Pain ripples through me once more.

"I do not," I mutter. Her words hurt far more than Jenine ever did. No, they hurt to the degree of Luis and Susan. People who told me they cared about me only to turn and hurt me with their words.

I never expected to hear any of this from her. Others maybe, but not Becks. But again, I'm wrong. Maybe our friendship wasn't meant to be forever, as we always said in our countless sleepovers.

"You clearly think we're all beneath you, but we're not. Not everyone can be the martyr saint you are," Becca screams and the waterworks slip past as she claws at my intentions. "Cassie, I didn't mean to say that," she says a minute later with regretful eyes.

But it's too late. The damage has been done.

"Cassie, I'm sorry. I didn't mean it. I don't know what took over me. I should have never said that to you."

She reaches for my hand, but I pull away before it's even possible. She's already chipped the small pieces that remained intact. I shake my head, stunned, looking at her in pure disbelief before I take off running, pushing past people without stopping.

I can't look at her. Not right now.

She's never spoken to me like this, and it hurts. It's quite telling, and she's wreaked havoc within my soul. For once, I feel alone in my world of pain. In the hell that is my life.

Her verbal attack broke me.

Their screams meet me, but I discard them. Hugh didn't once step in to stop her or even defend me. He berated me for speaking the truth about his sister. Becca assaulted me with words that hurt because they came from her.

The knower of my truth.

I don't stop until I'm out of the school and standing in the middle of the road, out of breath. My feet turn, needing to see Becca and Hugh, to see how far they made it. A small test to see how much they care about me.

Instead, I find them embracing and moving their lips in synchrony with one another. Since when have they been sleeping with one another? How long have I been their fool?

At a distance, I can hear a car honk but my heart bleeds to know how little I truly knew, my friend. To know how far she's changed since her first populars' party. But when it honks again, and the car comes into view in my peripheral vision, I turn towards it only to see it coming towards it.

My feet are left paralyzed as shock continues to thrum through my veins. The tires screech in an attempt to halt their racing speed. But the distance is too short.

This is it; this is how I die.

Becca

The second I saw Cassie's pain and the tears rolling down her cheeks, I regretted my words. I went too far in defending Jenine's honor, but Cassie doesn't know her. I do. Jeni isn't a villain.

I know the reason she's the way she is. The pain her parents brought her is one she's been unable to overcome, so popularity became her safety net. She simply takes far too much comfort in making others hurt as she does.

But it doesn't make me amiss about who she is and how much she's changed me without me knowing.

I've hurt Cassie. I can see it. The type of hurt the monsters bring her, but I'm not one like they are. I want to save her from them.

So I run after her with Hugh a close second behind. But doubt plagues me as I do. Am I doing the right thing or does she need space? How can I not know my best friend anymore?

Why am I even chasing after her when I'm not regretful of telling her the truth? I simply voiced out my conflicting emotions. Seems there has been a winner between the warring sides within me.

My steps slow down, and as I search for Hugh, I see him a few steps behind me. Clearly, he stopped before me. I'm willing to bet he was only truly chasing me after a while.

He walks towards me the moment our eyes connect and slips his hand into my own. Further questions plague me and my resolution to save Cassie further drowns. Why am I even bothering when she isn't even helping herself?

Hell, why do I even care? We're not the same anymore. Different standings in school. I'm a popular with Jeni as my best friend. Why do I care for Cassie, anyway?

"She's clearly delusional," Hugh whispers, and my heart is once more at a war on whether or not it agrees. I want to save her, but I also want to live my life. It's selfish but I want to play a blind eye. Everyone else does, so why can't I?

It's not like anything will happen.

My eyes catch sight of her running out of the school before Hugh pulls on my arm and wraps his arms around me. He gazes at me with pure affection.

"Screw Cassie. I'm done pretending Becky," he voices at me. "I want you and I'm done with us hiding."

He swoops in and kisses me senseless before whispering in my ear all the things he would love to do to my body. I giggle, getting swept off in the cloud of love and the thumping of my heart before connecting my lips with his once more. The horn of a car honking in the distance.

I'm sorry, Cassie, but for once it'll be about me. She needs to learn to save herself or find someone else to drag down. We're too different and it's best we cut our friendship here before we end up breaking each other.

Because I have no doubt, we hold that power over one another.

Rather, it end on a sour note than an irreparable one that kills us.

Smiling, and wrapped in one another, we walk in the opposite direction Cassie had with what sounds like screeching tires somewhere in the background. Either some people don't know how to drive or some idiot doesn't know the basic rules of walking. Regardless, who cares? I have everything I could want here with Hugh.

Someone New

♥

Brad

MY BIGGEST REGRET IN life has one name; Jenine Squire. A girl that is as fake as they come. A pretty little wrapper for a foul heart.

I only wish I had known before that she was the girl who broke my poor cousin's heart by confining her to the shadows. All because she's unable to accept who she is. Had I known she was the one that instilled all of my cousin's current insecurities, I never would have gone to her house.

Hell, I never would have slipped into bed with her.

But stupidly I ignored Grazella's advice that night and went with my friends to a classic populars' party from her old school. Clearly, she knew better. Regardless, I plan to rectify my mistakes and set this girl straight.

Better yet, I will make sure Jenine Squire never reaches out to Aze ever again. My cousin deserves better than a mean girl, and I'm happy she's moved on with someone else at her new school. Joy is too short a word to call the feeling I feel to know she's no longer moping over Jenine.

Now I simply have to make sure that girl never comes into our lives ever again.

"Brady, baby, I certainly wasn't expecting you," the mean girl says, flaunting in an all too sweet and preppy voice that grates my nerves. "Guess you simply couldn't get enough of me," she chirps with a smile.

My gaze trails over to her with nothing but vitriol and disgust that has her flinching. Good.

Many will see the small and utterly thin blond before me as nothing short of beautiful, but I know better than to be fooled by her false exterior. She's nothing but a pretty face with an ugly heart. One that wears far too much makeup even if it is impeccable and matches the skimpy outfit she has on because she has no curves. No meat to her bones.

I wouldn't be surprised if they diagnose her as anorexic, but it just goes to show that Jenine Squire is nothing but a fraud through and through. A pretty foil; I couldn't find any more unattractive even if I tried.

"Don't flatter yourself," I spit at her with contempt. She broke my cousin's heart without remorse and now I'm returning the favor on her behalf. "I'm simply here to tell you not to contact me again, and to walk the other way if we ever cross paths."

Her eyes squint as she scans me up and down with a shade of confusion coloring her blue irises that irk me. It's clear she's never been told no. Glad to be the first.

"I want nothing to do with you," I add with disdain.

"Yet here you are," she quips, proud of herself. "Playing hard to get..."

"In the slightest, only to warn you to stay away from me and my cousin," I cut her off, only to be met with a smirk.

"Baby, you insult me by daring to think that I, Jenine Squire, queen bee, who can have anyone she wants, will chase after anyone," she asserts in a sultry voice. "Even if they're as cute as you are."

"Grazella said you bore an ego the size of a mammoth. Guess she wasn't wrong."

Her eyes morph into an icy-cold glare the second my cousin's name leaves my lips. Glowering at me with unfiltered contempt as she attempts to intimidate me. But I'm not one to submit to some pretty girl's petty demands. A snarl covets her lips in a blaze of fury as my unbothered gaze remains unflinching.

"You tell Zelly that she better make quick work of accepting her place beneath me instead of throwing uncalled for tantrums before she truly makes me angry," she drawls out the threat with a vicious smirk. Anger boils my blood in a quick second. If this girl were a guy...

"My cousin doesn't need to hide in the shadows because some mean girl is far too afraid to come out of the closet. If anything, that's a you problem," I voice out. "There is nothing wrong with her and you will not make her feel like there is."

"I don't hide Brady. She's simply a nobody that should be grateful that I even want her," Squire remarks with a shrug.

"It's a good thing that *nobody* knows not to settle for the breadcrumbs an entitled spoiled, mean girl throws at her and has moved on to someone better," I declare in triumph as she seethes in her entitlement.

"Ratty patty is nowhere near my level and certainly not better."

"Beg to differ and she has a name, you know?" I note at her, but her careless expression at acknowledging my cousin's girlfriend is unsettling. "Grazella will never go back to you."

"That remains to be seen."

My head shakes as I respond, "The beauty of having loving parents who love you and accept you for who you are; means not settling for less than you deserve." Her lips press into a firm line, cheering me on to say my piece. "So, let this be your only warning to stay away from us both."

Jenine scowls at me with ire before turning on her heels and stomping away from me in a hurried stroll. A smile plasters on my face to see her walk away. Mission accomplished.

The mean girl will never think to bother my cousin or dare to ever contact me.

Swiveling on my own feet, I begin to make my way back to my car with relief flowing through me like a blanket. Coming here was the right choice.

A blur of brown draws my attention and I get whiplash by how fast I turn towards it at the instant connection I feel. My soul recognizes something and I'm met with an umbrella of brown hair. A common shade for the world's population, but it stole my breath away.

Anguish shone brightly in her russet brown eyes that I caught sight of for five seconds before she turned to face something behind her as an oncoming car blew its horn at her. Yet she seemed lost before granting it, her attention with tears bathing her beautiful cheeks.

Screeching sounds were heard as the driver tried to halt to a stop, but its rapid speed worked against him. Every coherent thought abandoned me as I raced towards her with a racing heart.

Cassie

My feet were rooted to the road the second I saw the car. My instincts too broken that I couldn't make the leap or attempt to save myself from the dire fate. Already resigned to the fact this is when I die.

My gaze locks with that of the frantic driver, a teacher, as he tries to prevent my demise. A feeling I wish I could feel. But that's been stolen by my demons.

I'm simply surv—

A gust of wind and a firm grip snap my frozen feet out of the way and onto the hard ground. The car scarcely missing me, but the pain in my leg was an obvious reminder that I'm both alive and was close to meeting my end. My eyes are desperate as I attempt to process the fact I'm still breathing.

I was so close to death. Turning to my right, I catch sight of my savior, and my heart races in the confinements of my chest. Uncertainty fills me as I'm unable to figure out if it's the fact I almost died or him. But I want to know.

Somehow, he landed on top of me and now hovered as his blue-gray eyes inspected me for injuries, as his light brown hair cascaded like a curtain, framing his face. I try to divert my gaze from his own, but my brain refuses to register the command. His eyes are simply so mesmerizing.

They steal your breath away...

"Are you okay?" The question slips past his beautiful, soft, pink lips and startles me out of my trance. Out of him. And back to reality.

"I think so," I force the words out of my mouth while fighting the wave of nerves that consume me. A foreign feeling as much as it is to have someone worry about me who doesn't know me.

It's astounding. I almost died and have a boyfriend. Yet I seem to be fawning over this guy.

But Hugh is a distant memory buried deep, somewhere deep in the fragments of my fractured mind. I'm so far from normal that I'm not even having the appropriate reaction to death. If anything, a small part of me craves it. Which is frightening.

"Good to hear," he answers, rolling off me and to the side before standing. I simply blink as my eyes get lost in the clouds above me. His hand comes into my line of sight and shock splays into my blood. "Here, let me help you up," he offers and I stupidly nod as I take a hold of his offered appendage.

He pulls me to my feet and I smile at the gesture. "Thank you," I mumble, trying not to revel at the feel of his hand on my own. Soft, strong, and reassuring. Our gazes lock and my heart flutters, numbing me to the now excruciating pain in my left ankle.

I'm captivated by his stare and want nothing but to lose myself in the depth of his irises. They glimmer with nobility and kindness, something unknown to me.

The feel of soft droplets on my skin alerts me to a shift in the weather.

"I'm glad to see you're okay," he murmurs, peeling his orbs of light away from me as he releases me from his hold. Intense throbbing registers in my brain and I take in a sharp breath to numb it.

It's a feeling I'm quite accustomed to.

"Thank you for saving me," I say before casting my eyes down in search of my bag while surviving the intense sting in my ankle.

"You're welcome," he replies, holding my bag out to me and I smile at its sight. "I believe this belongs to you," he adds, and I nod, taking possession of it. Our hands meet for a brief second, which leaves my body racked up with a tingling sensation I've never encountered. Not with Hugh or Luis or anyone.

It's different. Something I can't explain. Is this me liking him? Is this how it feels to like someone, or is it tied to the fact he just saved my life?

Wish I knew.

"Thank you," I speak through gritted teeth, attempting to be casual but failing miserably. Even as most of my weight is shifted onto my right leg.

Why am I so nervous about being around this guy? I've never been a fool with anyone. This guy is nothing more than a stranger who saved me. A cute stranger with light brown—

No! I can't go down that rabbit hole.

He saved my life, nothing more. That must be it. He saved my life.

But he's cute and saved my life. He is nothing like Hugo.

My subconscious resonates with words I have no interest in hearing. I'm dating Hugo, have been for months and he loves me and I love him...? Hurt vibrates through my body at the thought.

Why does it feel like such a lie?

If he loved you, then he would have saved you. Look

around you, Cassie, he isn't even here. Neither is Becca. You don't love him and simply care for him as a friend because he's your safety blanket.

Once more, my thoughts assault me violently with truths that destroy everything in me. My eyes wander to my surroundings in search of Becks and Hugh, only to prove my brain right. The memory of them embraced in each other's arms, kissing, as the car nearly ran me over hits me with force.

Now, they're nowhere in sight. Far away from saving me; from even coming to my aid.

How could I have been so stupid? How long have they been lying to me?

I try to place when things changed, and it circles back to Becca's first populars' party. Tears well up in my eyes at being deceived, and my retinas sting before they stroll down my cheeks till I'm bathed in them. More raindrops coat my skin and soon it's hard to distinguish which is staining my face.

"Are you okay?" My savior questions me and I recluse into myself, as always. He remains a stranger despite my liking of him.

"I'm fine," I utter, slapping my tears away. "Why wouldn't I be?" I ask, sarcasm dripping into my tone.

"You tell me," he answers my rhetoric question. "You seem to have a pretty good handle on almost getting run over, so what changed?" He pries deeper and, for the first time, my fight-or-flight instinct comes into play as a need to run fills me.

"I need to get out of here," I blurt out frantically. Desperate to keep my secrets, as if he'll pry them out. I know the effect they have on people. I can't drown others.

"Okay," he replies, and I turn on my heels to make my way elsewhere. I halt after the third step as pain ricochets from my ankle. My gaze travels down my leg to the appendage in question to find it severely swollen and bruised.

Another inconvenience. But nothing to be surprised

about. The teacher didn't even bother to stop and check in on me. Also, not a shock seeing it's rumored that he's sleeping with my bully.

How am I meant to make a clean getaway? Breathing in deeply, I begin my walk once more, needing to escape, but someone swifts by me, bumping into my side and knocking me off balance and onto the floor. I groan at the agony that flares inside me even more than before.

My savior is next to me in the blink of an eye, attempting to help me to my feet once more. I guess he was watching me. His arms slip behind my back and underneath my legs, carrying me bridal style as he catches onto my pain.

"You can put me down," I mumble, clinging to his neck.

"You're hurt. You have a swollen ankle that might be serious. My car is nearby, so let me take you to the hospital," he states, concerned, and I nod. No use fighting it. Walking is absolute torture and having him take me to get help will get me away from here quicker.

Away from Becca and Hugh. Exactly what I need.

He gets me into his car and buckles me in before he drives us to the hospital, where he makes me wait for him to leave the car. Unbuckles my seatbelt and carries me inside where we wait in a waiting room, eventually being seen. I'm informed that I tore my ankle ligaments in a terrible sprain.

To which I hardly pay any attention, unlike my savior.

We're given instructions and eventually left alone after receiving a set of crutches. I sigh in relief at the solitude, fighting the oncoming tears and numbness of being betrayed by the one I love the most. Had Becks just told me she wanted Hugh or had feelings for him; I would have left him. But to go behind my back?

"So, tell me, why were you crying?" My savior questions the second I'm discharged.

"I caught my best friend and boyfriend together," I confess, too tired to lie or fight. The lump in my throat grew by the second. "I thought I could trust..." *her.* The words trail off as the salty drops make their escape.

The truth lies that I could not care less about Hugh. I've never fully trusted him, but Becks? She's my best friend. My walking diary and I hers... Or so I thought.

"I guess not... I almost died and..." words fail me as emotion clasps tightly around me. Becks wasn't there to save me or even see if I was okay. She was lost in Hugh's arms for a second and then walked away.

"I'm sorry, but it's their loss, not yours," he expresses in a soft tone that comforts my aching heart even if I can't fully believe him. My eyes cast down, and he places his fingers beneath my chin to lift it up so our eyes meet mine. "They don't deserve your tears."

"Thank you," I mumble, uncertainly to be met with a warm smile.

"Now that I think about it, I don't even know your name," he chuckles and I join him with a wholehearted laugh because he's right. We don't know each other's name; neither of us has bothered to ask.

"Cassandra, but everyone calls me Cassie," I say, breaking the silence.

All my demons use my full name and I go by a nickname to disassociate from them.

"I'm glad I met you, Cassie," he answers with a smile.

"Likewise..." I reply, growing silent when it comes to his name.

"Brandon, but my friends call me Brad," he responds, and I nod.

"Likewise, Brandon."

"Brad."

"Likewise, Brad," I correct.

"Now where are we to go?" He asks a beat later and I shrug my shoulders, not knowing the answer.

"Anywhere but here," I say truthfully.

"Now that can be arranged," he conveys, slipping his arms underneath me to carry me once more bridal style.

"You know you don't have to carry me anymore. They did give me crutches," I mention with a giggle, grabbing them.

"I know," he replies as we leave the hospital.

Betrayal by a Friend

Becca

MY HEART TIGHTENS IN my chest and I can't help feeling something is wrong. Deep in my bones, I know it is. We've always known when something is wrong with one another. Still, I shove the feeling aside, remembering my last words to her.

Too much turmoil exists between me about it. I don't need more. I made my choice, part away from Cassie. We're too different.

Jeni and I are far similar and she's already a close friend. She can easily become my best friend if she isn't already. It's for the best.

"What's on your mind, Becky?" Jeni asks as Fanilea braids her hair from behind, ever the dutiful friend. If you ask me, she's far too obsessed with Jeni's words and needs to get her own life. Always circling around like a vulture.

"I was thinking about Cassie," I answer her truthfully.

"Please, that nobody doesn't deserve a second thought," Fanilea voices from behind and I glare at her.

"You don't know Cassie, so shove it," I snap at her.

"Hey, let's not fight for such an *insignificant* thing," Jeni chimes in before the bitch can even utter another word. "Fani, remember that Cassandra is still Becky's friend."

I roll my eyes at the silence that the little I'm everyone than everyone else eludes. People don't give her enough credit. If anything, she's far worse than Cassie claims Jenine is. A follower is always far more dangerous than a leader. They can never think on their own.

"Becky, Hugh told me of the little spat you two had," Jeni mentions, and I sigh, running my fingers through my auburn curls. "Care to talk about it?"

Turmoil plagues me with the need to scream it out and confess how I feel to someone else. I'm Cassie's vault and she's mine. But I need someone to trust and I know I can trust Jeni.

My mouth parts to let it all out, but my eyes catch sight of Fanilea and it clamps shut once more. That girl is an utter snake and clearly deranged. She would squash Cassie in a second and I won't allow it.

"Fani, I'm parched, go bring me a water," Jeni says dismissing her and so the obedient follower abides by her command without question. "She's gone now, talk to me," she coaxes the second the door closes.

"I love Cassie. We've been friends forever, but knowing what she goes through... it feels like it's like nothing matters but her pain. She tries so hard for it not to be that way, but just knowing..." the words tumble out of me without a second thought.

Doing my best to keep Cassie's secrets locked away and opening myself up to Jeni without a single reservation. Friends are there in the good and the bad. Cassie has shown me that. Jeni has proved herself to me.

"What do you mean?" Jeni's voice is soothing as she comes to sit next to me. "Tell me Becky, you can tell me anything," she persuades, and it's all I need to hear to give in to her request. Maybe she'll let go of what she has against Cassie if she knows her story.

"Cassie's stepfather is a monster who abuses her in every way you can imagine. Physically, emotionally, mentally, and, worse of all, sexually. Has been for years behind her mother's back," I confess as tears spill out of me.

Jeni looks at me shell-shocked and I push through.

"Cassie keeps it from her family because she knows it'll destroy them and she would never do such a thing to them. He's never hurt her siblings and she can't steal their dad away," I blurt out.

"What about Gilbert?" Jeni questions, and I sigh.

"He doesn't know. Only she, I, and now you do. But things aren't much better at his house. His wife is a narcissist who absolutely loathes Cassie and does nothing but berate her. Abuses her just like her stepdad, except Susan would never abuse her sexually. No, instead, the bitch neglects her profusely."

"So, Luis Anas..."

I nod before she can even voice out the words and break down.

"He's a monster as much as Susan is, but I don't know how to help her. I don't want to keep being her lifeboat and for us to both drown in the silence. I want normal and... I'm a terrible friend."

Jeni's arms wrap around me and she cradles me as my deepest secrets come out to the surface. "You are not a terrible friend, Becky. Cassandra was utterly selfish to tell you and force you to keep quiet."

"No, Jeni, she's an angel suffocating to keep everyone else happy and I'm the worst best friend because I can't be by her without thinking of me," I hiccup through the wracking sobs.

"Absolutely not. Cassie's emotional and mental state is not your burden to bear," Jeni coos at me. "That's on her. The reason I don't tell anyone about my parents is because no one will feel sorry for me. I'm the queen bee. Cassie is far too weak to understand such simple concepts, but that's not on you. That's on her."

"As her best friend, I should help her and be there for her. If anyone is weak, Jeni, trust me, it's me."

"No, I refuse to believe that, Becky," she states with a clear voice. "You know how I know that? Because my brother would never fall for a weak girl. Why do you think he loves you and not Cassie?"

"She's my best friend, and I had an affair with her boyfriend. How am I not an awful friend?"

"She stole my brother from you. All you did was simply get him back," Jeni assures me. Her words ring true, but a small part inside me still feels like they are a lie.

"It wasn't quite like that," I argue with her and get ready to talk about the subject, but the door to the room opens with Fanilea.

"What did I miss?" She questions and I turn away to hide my tearful face that no doubt ruined my make-up.

"Nothing, I accidentally poked my eye," I reply, without bothering to hide my annoyance.

"Whatever, Jeni, here's the water you wanted," Fanilea replies with an eye roll and our mutual friend nods.

"Come, Becky, let's fix your make-up so you can knock my brother off his feet when he sees you. My best friend needs to look perfect, *always*," Jenine says and I dip my head in agreement, already feeling lighter. Talking with Jeni really helped ease the weight over my chest.

Jenine

Schemes and plans immediately form in my head. Armed with Becky's newfound information, I have everything to meet my goal. The destruction of Cassandra Castillo is so close that I can taste it, and it's delicious.

Time ticked slowly, and it nearly drove me insane having everything within my reach, but I have to be careful with Becca. I'll risk losing her if I let her into my beautiful plans, unlike Fanilea. She's still too close to Cassie, but this will finally break the bond and get Becky to call me her best friend.

I can't waste time, or she'll go back to Cassie and apologize. The wedge I've been perfectly curating has to be pried open to make sure this split between them is permanent. I've finally got what I wanted and it will stay that way.

A knock on the door and the utter lack of waiting for a response before it's being opened lets me know Hugh is here. Late like always when needed, but at least he's here to take Becky out. At least he's here now, so I can begin my plans of destruction.

"Jeni, I'm taking my girlfriend now," he orders like the utter child he is.

"She's been ready for over two hours, knucklehead," I happily inform him. Hugh's eyes narrow on me, but I don't even grant him my acknowledgment. Already bored with him. Wasting my precious time with his utter nonsense.

Fabrications begin in my flawless brain, while meaningless conversation starts around me. I'll need to talk with Susan Pearce and tell her all about how Cassandra is sputtering lies about her, such as the fact that she beats on her. I'll also have to get proof of her relationship with her stepfather because I don't for a second believe anyone could be interested in Cassie without her provoking.

She's a martyr and those are the worst. But I'll unveil her. Expose her to the entire world. I simply need to see how to do so without Becky knowing it was me. She was very clear to note only we knew of Cassandra's secrets.

Becca is naïve to believe the lies her future ex-best friend sputters, but I'm not. I'll lose her if she finds out it came from me, but if I start it and simply do nothing to stop it... then she can't fault me.

"Jeni, they've left," Fanilea informs me, and I grin at her sight. "What?"

"We're going to destroy Cassandra Castillo and you'll take

the credit," I answer her triumphantly.

"What do I need to do?" She questions with a smile, like the obedient puppy she is. The perfect follower.

"Get your phone. We're going to Cassandra's house to get proof the skank is sleeping with her stepfather so we can expose her to the school tomorrow."

"Anything for you, Jeni," she replies dutifully, and I grace her with a hug.

"Thank you. I notice Fani and out of them all, you're my favorite," I compliment her and she nearly faints. Good. "Which is why this will remain a secret between you and me. Becky can't know about it."

"Of course, I have my phone. Shall we get going?"

"I trust you to do this on your own. I have to go meet with Susan Pearce to tell her about the horrid things Cassandra has been sputtering behind her back."

"I won't disappoint you," she rambles off in glee before racing out of my room.

Your time has come, Cassandra Castillo. I got you now.

Cassie

I wake up with the biggest smile, remembering the previous day with Brad. Although I almost died, I got to meet him, a new shining light, and for that, I couldn't be more thankful. Spending time with him was a small reprieve from hell and a piece of heaven that I've never had.

It's worth the fright my mother had when I arrived home on crutches. Thankfully, Brad was with me and explained everything, which in the end calmed her down. She expressed her gratitude by inviting him to dinner. Something the monster did not like, and I came to know when he found a moment alone with me before my mom settled into my room, worried I would need anything during the night.

Silent tears were spilled that night while she dreamed. The pain was ever so great and the pressure was all too suffocating.

But they were dry by the time we woke up and she called my dad to drive me to school because she couldn't be late to work. I kept silent during the entire journey, not wanting to go now that Becks and I... were so uncertain. But I had no choice.

My mother would never allow me to miss school. Even when sick, she sends me unless the doctor tells her I'm to stay home, or the nurse sends me home. Olivia Castillo will not have her children miss school if she can help it.

Dad didn't bother striking up a conversation, far too preoccupied with work, which I understood. I always did for him and mom. Neither was at fault for my hell. They didn't know the weight I carried in order for them to remain happy. They're simply oblivious.

I smile at him when we arrive at school, far too accustomed to masking my pain, and wish him a good day at work. He has me promise to call him if I need anything and leaves after I nod and close the door.

Bracing myself for the strenuous day ahead, I take in a deep breath and walk into what is as close to a sanctuary as I have. People whisper and laugh as I pass by them on my crutches. The glances they throw my way nearly drive me insane and frustration pricks at my skin.

It all becomes too much. It's like a rope wrapped around tightly around my neck and I'm desperate for escape. My eyes scan the hallway in search of one, and I breathe in relief at the sight of a bathroom.

I seek refuge in it and breathe in relief the second I step in. But horror grapples my heart at the sight that greets me. Photos of me splay all around the walls.

My hell haunts me in its present form. Multiple images of my stepfather and me in compromising positions that differ so much from the truth litter the room. Pictures of me and Susan that paint me in a horrible light share the spotlight with the monster I fear the most.

The populars. This is their work. Becca told them. She told them everything and they've warped my truths like I knew they would. No one ever believes me!

She was the only one to know.

Tears flood out as I struggle with my crutches to pull every print off the walls with every intention of throwing them into the trash. I need to get rid of this. How many have seen it already? Oh god!

Life is only going to get worse. Why does everyone hate me? Everything here is a lie. My deepest guarded secrets were twisted into lies and exposed for everyone to see to serve as judge and jury.

What if my family caught wind of this? Teachers? Will they do anything? They're going to break us all apart, and I'll be the only one to blame.

Heaviness clamps around my heart as the silence is deafening.

The door opens and I swivel, attempting to hide the hundreds of photos. My eyes meet with those of my tormentor who smiles like the wicked being she is. Fear thrums in my ears as I struggle to dominate the panic inside me and get my instincts to work properly for once.

But they don't.

I remain frozen in place.

"Welcome to your end, Cassandra Castillo," Jenine Squire says with the biggest of smiles before she closes the door.

The soft click of a lock greets my ears and I leap into action too late to open the damn door. Discarding the crutches to the side in search of escape, yet the knob refuses to open.

My feet slip, and I fall on my injured. A scream ripples out of me from the agony and I come face-to-face with the foul smell of toxic chemicals and a note.

"See you in hell, Cassandra," I read out as a hackling

cough possesses me because of its powerful stench. My hand clamps over my mouth and I try to use my long sleeve shirt to keep from breathing in the smell of death, but the need for air overpowers me. My arm falls limp and darkness takes a close hold of me as I fall into the arms of sleep, vulnerable to my demons.

I'm startled awake by the arms of a custodian brutally shaking me. Confusion and terror intertwine in my blood and I jump to my feet, grappling for my bag and crutches, fearful to be hurt. The look of the woman is one of absolute wariness as I scramble out of the bathroom at full speed.

Despite my hoarse throat, I choke on the fresh air that greets me as I stumble into the hallway and out the doors to the outside as the bell rings and people crowd out of the classroom. Navigating my way around them proves difficult as they push and shove me until I meet the cool air of the outdoors.

I'm oblivious to my surroundings or steps as I crash into some kids that knock me into the mud. Horrid names are called out and getting on all fours, I come to stand with adrenaline coursing through my veins, numbing the pain in my ankle. But I never get to my feet as I'm shoved into the ground by other students.

Forceful kicks and agonizing blows are thrown at my wrangled body by my classmates. No one moving a single finger to help me. All joining in. Because no one goes against the populars. They all wish for her good graces.

They all want Jenine Squire's attention and I'm nobody but a means to an end for them.

The day progresses terribly slow, but grows in horror as everyone becomes my enemy. My eyes search every set of eyes in the crowd, always hoping to find Becca they're coming to save me, but she never appears. Her perfect auburn curls never come into sight.

The monster picks me up that day and I'm forced to allow his lips to kiss mine, despite me having them in a firm line. His hand lingers on my thigh the entire way home and dread fills my stomach.

No one is home. I know it, and it's only confirmed when we pull up into the driveway and the front door closes behind us. His hand clamps over my mouth as screams crackle at my throat and he takes me like always.

Against my will.

Confession

♥

Becca

MY PHONE BUZZES INCESSANTLY on Hugh's nightstand along with his own, and it irritates me to no end. There was a reason we didn't go to school. It was to spend the day wrapped up in one another.

It vibrates again and I push him to the side to see what has everyone so worked up that they need us. Snatching my phone off the bed table, I unlock the screen and click on the first social media notification I have. Horror grapples at my heart as pictures of Cassie flood my feed.

Rumors surround her, claiming she's having an illicit affair with her stepfather behind her mother's back. Unfounded lies about the treacherous daughter she is to Susan, who does nothing but love her. All fabrications of the truth and none bearing an ounce of Cassie's true story.

In vain hope, I jump to my other apps and find the same thing. Every social media platform I know and use is berating her. My heart breaks at the bashing of the angel I've called best friend for years.

Where did this all come from? No one knows of Cassie's secrets but me! Me... and... Jeni.

By the time my mind is done processing, I'm slamming Jenine's door open in search of answers. Fanilea jumps from the bed completely startled as my so called new best friend looks at me with confusion. But appearances lie.

She was the only one I told about Cassie's story. She had to have done this. Broke my promise of being Cassie's vault and she mine.

"What is this, Jenine?" I demand, with boiling anger. "Why is everyone saying Cassie lays down with her father willingly when we both know that is nothing but a lie!"

"Becky, what did I do?" She dares to play the victim with furrowed eyebrows. People lie. Susan Pearce is the perfect example of that.

"Don't play stupid with me, you're the only one I told! Cassie would never tell anyone!"

"I promise you, I told no one of what we spoke! I would never betray you," she snaps at me with utter outrage. But she fails to realize she won't fool me. I'm not blind to the truth anymore. She wanted to destroy Cassie.

"I don't believe you! How long did you have this planned? Were you using me all along? Hugh too? To destroy my best friend!"

"Don't raise your voice at Jeni!" Fanilea jumps to her defense, ever the dutiful follower. Pathetic. "Much less for a nobody like Cassie, who is nothing but a whore who is sleeping with her mother's husband. Who does such a horrid thing?"

"You know nothing!"

"Please, I know everything," Fanilea snarls. "One talk with Susan Pearce and glance into her window and it was quite clear what type of person Cassandra Castillo is. Only fair, I expose her to the world."

Her words leave me awestruck, and I stumble back. It wasn't Jeni? It was her?

"Please, you would say anything for Jenine," I argue, not quite convinced she was the mastermind of this nightmare.

"You're right. I would do anything for Jeni and destroying Cassandra for her is my utter pleasure. I knew she would do nothing with what you told her because she cares for you, but I don't have the same problem."

"You heard our conversation?" I question.

"How you sobbed like a baby because of Cassandra's lies? Of course, I did. The leech lied to you, Becky. She was never abused, and now the world knows the truth. You're welcome," she barks, and I turn my gaze to Jeni, who remains oddly silent.

"Fani, how could you betray Becky like that?" Jeni inquires with an oddly soft voice resembling weakness. Jenine Squire does not show such vulnerabilities. It's unorthodox of her.

"Cassandra lied to her and would eventually come for you, Jeni. I couldn't let Becky believe such fabrications and turn against you. I love you both," Fanilea utters with emotion and disbelief, claws at me. Cassie wouldn't lie to me, I know it. This bitch just spread lies about my best friend.

"Cassie didn't lie to me! I know it," I dispute and plead with Jeni through a gaze to believe me. "Jeni, please. Help me set the record straight. The school will ruin her. Help me stop these lies, please. I know there's bad blood between you two, but please don't let lies ruin her. You're better than this."

She sighs but nods. "I promise to do whatever I can to help you, Becky," she assures me, and hope flickers inside. Jenine owns the school and if anyone can help Cassie right now after Fanilea's absurd lies, it's her.

I'll do everything to save Cassie. We may no longer be friends, but I still care for her and will do just about anything to ease her suffering. I just hope she can hold on till Jeni can fix this for her.

Cassie

Things only deteriorate with the pass of time. Everyone

ignores my torment like always, or maybe it is that the mask never slips before the innocent. My only safe place from the bigger monsters is no more, and both of them only grow in power. Knowing now more than ever that I'll never be able to escape them.

My only reprieve is the times Brad takes me out to spend time together and his texts throughout the day. But I'm not naïve enough to believe it'll last forever. Eventually, he'll see too. I'm not worth it and leave. He'll hate me too.

I know it. Everyone does.

Still, I allow myself to live in the present because he's my relief amidst all the hate. My only friend who asks too many questions that I can't bring myself to answer.

But I always dismiss or turn the conversation because now more than ever, I know I can't trust anyone. I thought I could trust Becks, but she went and told my enemies, who warped my story to fit their narrative. Added to my already raging hell.

Created a brand new demon for me to face. Every dark thought I've ever had spewed out of my classmates' mouths. A personal catalyst to break me further when I thought I could break no more.

As always, God serves to prove me wrong.

It takes close to three weeks of constant agony for me to seek a breath of fresh air. To scream out in dear agony at the top of my lungs in the water of my bathtub after yet another night of being visited by the monster and another day where Becca does nothing to come to my rescue. I cave to the need for freedom and scroll through the dead of the night for my dad's number.

My breathing is shallow, and sobs are rippling out of me as I wait for him to answer my call. His wife might still be one of my monsters, but by now I need one of them gone. I can't deal with the one here.

"Hello?" His drowsy voice rings out and I snivel at the sound. My heart far too fractured to find the words to explain everything to my dad. The one person I fully believe will save me from Luis.

"Daddy," I weep into the night.

"Cassie, what's wrong?" My dad's startled voice echoes in my ear as I continue to bawl my eyes out. "Sweetie, talk to me."

"Daddy, I need you to save me," I beg. "I don't want him to touch me anymore," I mutter.

"You don't want who to touch you?" He questions like I knew he would.

"Luis," I breathe out. "I don't want him to hurt me anymore."

"Hurt you how, Cassandra?"

"I'm tired of being raped at home. Tired of being bullied at school. I'm tired of paying for the broken plates." As another sob escapes me, I trail off. "I need you to save me, please. Daddy, I'm worn out."

"Where are you?"

"My room," I answer, my exhaustion bleeding through.

"Lock the door and let no one in. Daddy is coming to get you. That bastard won't hurt you anymore, I promise," he assures me, and for the first time in my life, I cry in relief. "Susan, where are the keys?"

"Gilbert, slow down. It's the dead of the night," the stepwitch's voice is but a whisper in the background that isn't enough to break through my joy to know I'll escape one of the three. Then I'll tell him all about his wife, like Becks always told me to do.

Dad will keep me safe. I know it. Then it can be him and me while mom remains with my siblings and the monster.

"My daughter needs me. I'm going to her," he spits at her, and the clinging sound of metal alerts me to the nearness of my escape from hell.

"You're far too angry to go on your own. I'll go with you," she argues with him, but even knowing she's coming does little to evaporate my relief.

"I'm on my way. Lock the door, I'll be there soon," he reaffirms me and I simply nod as the line goes dead. A smile creeps up my face as I rise from the floor feeling lighter than ever, and lock my bedroom door.

I'll finally be free. The silence won't kill me anymore. Someone cares about me and will save me.

I drop to the ground and rest my head against my bed, waiting for my dad to come and rescue me. Tears continue to stroll down my cheeks as everything replays in my mind and I dwell on how bad things had to get before I sought further help than Becks. A mistake because my emotional and mental state wasn't and isn't her responsibility.

Yet by telling her and binding her to the silence with me, I made it so. Maybe after dad saves me, I'll be able to apologize and with time we can renew our friendship. Once she abandons her friendship with my tormentors.

It's the only way I could ever harbor the idea of us being friends again. Because right now, trust is broken, and that's the most fragile and difficult thing. Especially for a person far too withered like me.

Sleep wraps around me tightly in a security blanket for once as I wait for my savior to come. In a few hours, I'll be free. All it took was my confession.

"Cassie! Cassie, sweetie, open the door!" My mom's urgent cries startle me awake and I see the pooling sun rays of light flooding my room.

Joy fills me at the thought of my dad being here, and I spring onto my feet, racing to the door. Flipping the lock, I slam the door open to face my mom.

"Is dad here?" I question with glee, and her eyes grow somber. Something isn't right. Dread courses through my veins. "He was coming to see me. Is he here?"

"Sweetie, your father and Susan were in a car accident last night," she informs me with tearful eyes. "They didn't make it," she adds and my heart splinters open at her words.

No. No. No. No. No. Dad can't be dead. He can't be dead.

He promised to save me. No! He can't be dead after I sought him out for help.

Grief runs rampant inside me and tears at my insides as my limbs fail me. I fall into a heaping mess onto the floor as sobs take a hold of me and my mother holds me tightly in her arms in comfort.

Oh god, I wanted Susan gone and killed my dad with her. I'm a monster.

Guilt eats at me and I'm utterly destroyed, as is every inkling of hope to escape. My chest feels heavy as the weight of the world lies on my shoulders and I scream at the top of my lungs.

No sound echoes out of my throat as I swallow the silent screeching and replace them with sobs over the one parent who could take me away from all of this. The agony of losing my father only grows with time, and I'm only allowed four days away from school as funeral arrangements are made.

Brad makes certain to visit me the second he hears of my loss, but he doesn't get how great it is. Nor does he get how it's all my fault. No, to him, this is just another child losing her father, but it's more than that. It's an angel giving up its last hope and ready for death to take her.

It's me giving up on life.

"Cassie, I'm sorry for your loss. I know how it feels."

I shake my head at him as I remain huddled in the chair of my desk, resting my chin on my knees. "No, you don't, because you didn't kill your dad. I'm responsible for him being gone. It's all my fault," cries rip from me and his arms wrap around me like my mom's have done most of the day.

"No, it isn't your fault. These things happen and he wouldn't want you to be sad," he coos, stroking my hair. "I lost my dad four years ago and nearly lost my mom soon after," he confesses. "So I get the pain you're in."

My sorrow only grows at his words because he's wrong. I know from heaven or wherever my dad is that he's weeping. He wanted to save me and now he's gone because I couldn't handle a bit of pain.

By the next day, we're burying my dad and his witch of a wife. No one was as broken about it as me. They all had content and happy lives, while mine had nothing but agony. Even Becks attended and offered her condolences, but they meant little when she came with the Squire family as Hugh's girlfriend.

In two weeks, I was notified that my father had left everything he owned to his children in equal parts. Mine included a college fund and the rest of my inheritance wouldn't be available to me until I turned twenty-one, which was a lifetime away, and doubtful that I would even reach that age.

Everything went downhill from there. My will to fight was no more and completely eviscerated. I only attended school because of my mother forcing me to, but really I didn't want to go. The kids already made my life a living hell and only chanted about how I killed my father.

How he found out about my affair with my stepfather and was so ashamed he rather be dead than have a daughter like me.

Utterly heartless, as always.

They were my demons in the day, but my stepfather remained the monster of the night, having gotten more aggressive and brazen now that my dad was gone. I quit spending so much time with Brad, wanting to spare him from my loss that now seemed evidently close with as many blows as I took.

No doubt death would claim me soon. And hard to be with someone who doesn't understand the depth of your pain. More so when you can't tell him because it would only mark him for death and suffering like it did my dad.

Kids had already called me by every name in the book, but the day I came back from my father's passing, they cut my hair in a terrible pixie cut and got beaten bloody. Mom questioned me about it and, as always, I came up with an elaborate lie that made her suspicious. But that went out the window when she got a call from the school because of the lies they spread about me doing something unacceptable.

She wrote it off to me acting out from dad's death and I never bothered to correct her having learned my lesson. I didn't need to pop her bubble of joy by telling her the truth or the lie I kept getting harassed about.

That I, Cassandra Castillo, slept with her husband with consent. Nor did she need to know about the countless fake pages students had created where I supposedly prostituted myself online. No, she didn't need to know that.

I was drowning like never before with no one to aid or run to. I had no one. My dad was dead.

No one stood up for me or even stood by me; always siding with my aggressors. I was groped by guys and eventually; they started pressing their lips over mine against my will just like the monster. Mockery and laughs ensued soon after and were done at my expense. I was even given money by the same teacher, who nearly ran me over in hopes I would open my legs for him.

Further sites were created where the sole purpose was to insult me and create new false rumors about me. Always forwarded to my email despite how many times I changed it.

Leaving me officially broken and beyond anyone's repair.

Shattered

Cassie

I RACE HOME AFTER yet living another nightmare at school, and thank the god I really don't even believe in that my stepfather isn't home. Thankful that I'm able to cry in solitude for a few minutes. I run up to my room and shut the door behind me, not even bothering with the lock.

It won't help me either. The monster always finds a way in. Maybe one of these days he'll finally be merciful and reunite me with my father.

My bag finds its way onto the floor, and I pace the room as tears blur my vision. I run my fingers through my now short hair and despair runs me rampant at the loss of knowledge of what to do.

Somehow my feet take me to my computer in hopes the answer can be found there. I click on my email and open it, hoping to see at least one message from a college to get me to hold on. Perhaps one of the abroad programs I signed up for actually replied and I'll be free from them all.

Ignoring the hateful mail in my inbox, I scroll through until the name of a university pops up. Without thinking it twice, I open the email and click on the link that will take me to the university's homepage for more information. Disappointment greets me as I discover it to be a lie.

No school's web page pulls up. Instead, all the pages created to berate me do. Horror colors my face in the vague reflection of my screen as their words assault me. Against my better judgment, I read through the comments.

Their stupid opinions break me more so. These people don't know me, yet they hate me. Maybe I am at fault for everything.

"I wish she died!"

"She sleeps with her stepdad. What a slut!"

"Her father probably found out, and that's why he's dead."

"Her dad killed himself because his daughter is such a whore."

"Cassandra Castillo is such a joke! No wonder Hugh left her for Becca."

"Why can't she die? Like why can't she put a bullet through her skull, hang herself, or take some pills? I hope she's reading this and knows how much we hate her."

"I know, right? Her mom probably regrets having her., I know I would. What kind of slut sleeps with her mother's husband?"

"Like morals, where?"

I pull away from my desk, unable to keep reading the horrid things they're spewing about me. Why do they hate me so much? I've kept to myself all these years and have not once thought about hurting anyone.

I've done everything right. Yet I only keep getting punished.

How can any of these people throw around suicide so easily at me? What have I ever done to them for them to wish me harm? I've done my best to be kind because I know the pain of hell.

I've been nice to everyone I've ever encountered, yet they're hanging onto the lies Jenine and her populars have told about me. How can they?

Their cruelty truly knows no bounds. Jenine Squire is a virus that infects all those around her with her hate, including Becca. Otherwise, I wouldn't have my classmates harassing me. More so with my father being gone.

He died and they beat me bloody after cutting my hair. They don't get that he died because he was going to save me from the monster. I told him the truth, and it cost him his life.

I don't sleep with my stepfather. He is not my lover.

He's my abuser. My rapist. I only keep silent for the sake of my family.

And I'm tired of them twisting everything; it hurts. It's like daggers to my battered soul to know no one will believe me and if I were to speak now, there's no doubt they would side with my aggressor.

A ping draws my attention back to the computer screen. A new message.

"Hey, Cassandra Castillo. I dare you to quit burdening everyone and kill yourself once and for all. Spare us all from having to breathe the same air as you."

The words play in a loop in my head. Kill myself. Quit burdening everyone. Spare them the pain.

It becomes as clear as water.

Killing myself. An escape from the pain. Killing myself will end the pain.

This is the only way to make it stop. To be free. I can no longer take it. I'm tired of living. I've done my penance.

A picture of Becca and me glimmers as the sun hits it and I caress the frame it's in. My heart agonizing over her as well.

She was my best friend.

How could she do this to me? Betray me... I thought our friendship was forever. We swore it. Sealed it with a pinky promise when we were kids. Yet it seems our vow only meant something to me...

Otherwise, I wouldn't be alone and broken. Being assaulted left and right. A punching bag that no one is willing to catch when it collapses but throw away.

I thought I knew her... I opened up to her about my

demons, my every doubt and fear... I completely trusted her. I believed she would forever be there for me. The only one who would remain by my side, no matter what.

Be there rain or sun. Clear skies or thunderstorms. But I was wrong; I trusted the wrong person, and it hurts so much.

Why did she have to lie to me? Hide her true feelings and who she was? Deceive me in such a way that would finally drown me in my despair...

What did I ever do to her? What did I do that drove her to ruin my life so viciously?

I wish I knew so I could go back in time and remedy whatever hurt her. Fix what I did wrong. So, I would have never lost her to begin with. Her betrayal is killing me from the inside out, and I don't have it in me to keep fighting. I'm tired, so tired of fighting to simply breathe.

I don't want to think or feel her betrayal anymore. It torments my heart far too much. She knows the truth, yet she still lets everyone sputter lies and warp the truth of my story. Condemning me further into the hell I already know and creating a new one for me at school.

Robbing me of any haven free of pain.

And I don't want to keep worrying. Looking over my shoulder. Not at home and not at school. I don't want to fear anyone anymore. I just want to be free and know peace. I want the pain to stop...

Mom will be okay. She'll have *him* and my siblings. Dad's already gone and I'll get to see him again. And I lost Becca a long time ago, the moment she went to that stupid populars' party. Brad will forget about me quickly. After all, I'm no one. Nothing more than a burden on everyone else.

They will be okay. Better without me. I won't be missed.

I need the tears to cease. The pain to become numb. I don't want to... to... I don't want to keep breathing. Not when it hurts so much.

I don't want to live.

My soul craves peace. One only death can provide. I need

everything to stop. The voices, the bullying, the abuse. I want to be free.

No one cares for me anymore. They won't miss me. Everyone will be better off without me, like those stupid sites say.

Their hateful words come back to haunt me and drown me even further in the spiral of dark thoughts. It's as if they were all right here with me, yelling them at me. I cradle my knees to my chest as I pull on my hair, needing them all to shut up. Needing the madness of my hell to disappear.

But it doesn't. It further grows. Ignoring it is nowhere near in mind. Because it's impossible to do so. I'm not strong enough.

The feeling of ending it all only grows even further. I should just listen to those who seek my death. They're right, I'm nothing but a terrible human being. I should just end it all and be done with it.

I once thought I had Becca by my side, but even she left me in the end. Betrayed me for them. Left me behind to be in the spotlight and be... normal. Something I'll never be. I'm far too broken.

Tears blur my vision to no end as they pour out of me like a fragmented dam as I contemplate my options for escaping this world permanently. The dark void inside pulling me underneath its beautiful promise of death.

I don't want to go to school tomorrow just to be tortured with their lies and fists. I don't want to endure another night or moment in his presence, or worse underneath his heavy body. I can't do this anymore.

My only escape is to disappear... disappear into the darkness to escape the pain that consumes me daily. The price is far too high this time around and I can't bear it. I'm tired of being the one to pay for the broken plates.

That's the only answer to my problems. My only escape to the pain that has me in a tight hold, unwilling to let me go. Death. So I won't have to endure another day in this hell. My only way out is to stop breathing.

End my life.

I'll just be ridding the world of its error. Having been born. It just brought everyone far more pain and death than I'm worth. I'm a mistake and I need to correct it. My tears will cease and I'll be at peace. Who cares if my heart stops beating in the process? No one has cared for me before and they won't now.

With that in mind, I scroll back to the many suggestions given to make it definitive. My family doesn't own a gun and I don't know the first thing about using it, so a bullet is out of the question. I don't think I own something long enough to hang myself, nor do I know where, so that's out, too.

Drowning is already an everyday thing and I would like to go without the pressure for loss of air. So, pills it is.

I go in search of the pain medication I got for my leg months ago and a glass of water. Less than five minutes later, I'm back in my room, looking between the two and the computer screen.

More pings reach my ears and my decision cements. I record all my goodbyes on my phone and leave the device unlocked so they can find them. But in case they don't pay mind to it, I write them letters to let them know they aren't at fault for my choices and I wish them the best life.

I write one for Becks too.

Staging them neatly on my desk, I uncap the bottle of painkillers and down them with the help of water. This is the right choice. I'm broken and I need the pain to stop. This is the only way.

I abandon them both by my desk and head to the balcony annexed to my bedroom. If this is truly the end, then I want to leave with the sun warming up my skin. Looking at the sky above in peace. I pull myself onto the railing and sit over it, feeling a soft breeze on my arms.

My eyes glance one last time to my room, the bearer of my hell, before locking up with the clouds above me. A wave of exhaustion fills me and my eyelids grow heavy. I can feel the slowing down of my heartbeat. The end is near.

A smile creeps up my face. I'll be free from my hell and my family won't be broken by the truth. We'll all be happy. Me, in death, free of the silence, and them in life.

My hands hold me steady for my last moments of breathing as the opioids make the desired effect on my body. My skin grows clammy and cold as my breaths come out shallow and slow.

Confusion sets as I think about a life free of pain. Does it truly exist? What if I never find it? No, I have to. I'll go to a better place.

Mom believes in God and he'll welcome me into his kingdom after everything he's put me through. I'll be away from the monsters and all the agony.

Everyone I love comes to mind, along with the tears they'll shed. My heart throbs painfully in my chest at the thought, and for a moment, I regret my choice. But then I remember the monsters and demons I face in life and my remorse evaporates.

Instead, I pray for a faster escape. I can't handle the aching of living anymore.

Steps alert me to someone's presence and, curious, I open my closed eyes to say goodbye to the monster. He steps out to the balcony and laughs echo in my ears. Soft and maniacal laughs that belong to a demon, but the world around me is nothing but a blur.

Two people. Both girls. That's as much as I know in my delirious state.

Perhaps it's the angels taking me away. My eyes lock with theirs.

"Die, Cassandra Castillo," she mutters, standing before me and pushing me backwards. My hands come loose from the railing and my arms flop as I fall into blackness. Everything happens in slow motion as I fall towards certain death.

My last seconds feel as an eternity as my body comes to crash against our family car. Every bone in my body contracts and rippling agony ripples through me while maniac laughter can be heard from my balcony.

My sights set on the sky as I'm met with paralyzing pain. Birds fly above me. White doves. A sunny day and doves to see me off. I would die on a sunny day. The irony of it all. My consciousness drifts into the darkness while my thoughts settle on how ironic my death is.

So much turmoil within me and none in the outer world. No rain or storm like the one inside me. Just a regular day with the sun shining at all its might.

Goodbye, cruel world, you're finally getting your wish. I'll cease to live and a blunder will be fixed, how it should have been from the start.

Jenine

Coming here to warn Cassandra away from Becky had seemed like a splendid idea. But as Fani's deranged laughter meets my ears as we our look at Castillo's wrangled body shattered above a car, not so much. The goal was simple; come and strike utter terror in her for Becca to let her go.

Nothing is simple anymore. Cassandra Castillo is now dead and I know the moment MY best friend hears about it, I'll lose her once more to this utter leech. Her death should bring me relief and happiness. I should be feeling triumphant.

I finally got what I wanted. The destruction of Cassie.

But I feel none of the sort. No, I feel anger and despair. Fanilea just killed her without a second thought, despite the fact we found the empty pill bottle and glass. She was already ending it all.

Now she's implicated us in the bitch's murder. Will Cassandra Castillo ever truly stay out of my way?

I feel nothing for her loss. It doesn't grant me my parents' love or acceptance. She's never posed so much a threat to steal Becky away from me as now, and I won't have it.

If my best friend were to ever find out the part I played in Cassie's death, she'll hate me. I'll lose her. Damn Fanilea and damn the dead girl.

"She's dead," Fanilea squeals in delight, resembling a seal. I glare at her, not even caring anymore that she pushed the menace off the balcony railing. The past can't be changed, but I can prepare for the future.

Keep things going my way.

"You pushed her off and killed her," I mutter displeased, granting her my attention and peeling my eyes off Cassie. Seeing the life drain out of her haunts me, but not enough to break down in tears. She got what she reaped.

"For you," Fanilea says, confused. "Cassandra Castillo stood between you and your happiness and now she can't," she adds, reeking of sincerity.

My gaze diverts from her and bounces around the balcony, my skin itching to run before I get caught. Anyone can come at any moment.

"She was already going to kill herself. If anything, you interrupted her suicide and turned it into murder. Made me your accomplice," I inform her while also waving her off.

"I'm sorry but she deserved it and now we're certain she's gone," Fanilea sputters nonsense.

"We have to go before we get caught. I have no intention of going to jail for her death, no matter how much she deserved it. Now!"

I snap my fingers when she remains still. The second I do, she races to my side like the obedient puppy she is and we're on our way out of her room. My eyes catch sight of her desk and the neatly piled letters left there when she chose to finally do us all a favor.

Front and center is a pretty white envelope with angel wings and the name *Becks* stands tall.

Rage bubbles in my blood at its sight. Cassandra Castillo will not steal my best friend from her grave. Not if I can help it. I snatch the letter off the desk and stomp towards the door and out of the bitch's house.

"Rest in hell where you deserve Cassandra," I mutter as I pass by her body with Fanilea in tow.

Mother's Grief

♥

Narrator

LESS THAN TEN MINUTES later, Olivia arrived home from work to find something had fallen over the family car. A curse rippled over her as she contemplated costs from the distance. But as she neared it, she saw what it was. Cassie.

She nearly crashed at the sight as a scream rippled out of her.

Hardly remembering to set her own vehicle in park, she threw herself out and ran to her daughter's bloody body. Despair coated the air as her hands scrambled to search for a pulse. Any sign of life, no matter how small.

She nearly collapsed in relief when she found it. Faint, but there.

In less than fifteen seconds, she was on the phone calling for an ambulance, and about seven minutes later; they arrived. The sound of their sirens, deafening in the background as they pulled the broken girl off the car and onto the stretcher to load her up with her mother taking possession of her hand.

Climbing into the back with her and leaving with the paramedics as they breezed through the streets. Tears blinded her as much as her own terror as they made their way to the hospital. Her heart dropped when Cassie flat-lined on the way there.

Screams nearly toppled out of her as they performed CPR on her and brought back her near to none heartbeat. Pain embraced her soul and grappled tightly at her heart, nearly squeezing her own life away.

The doors burst open, and they were met by doctors as they unloaded Cassie back onto the floor. Her hand slipped from her grasp and Olivia nearly lost her sanity. She sought to retrieve it and accompany her through the maze of hospital hallways, but was held back.

Agonizing cries clawed their way out of her as she fell into a numb mess. "CASSIE!" Liv had been torn open by Cassie's decision to end it all to seek an escape from her pain. She was at a complete loss for the causes that led her daughter to attempt against her life. Unaware that even that decision had been stolen away by her demons.

If only there were a way for the dead to communicate with the living, then the truth would be shared. Cassie's silence would be broken and Olivia would bear the chance to grant her the peace she sought in death. But the veil between life and death stood strong and impeded the snatching of the veil laid over all their eyes.

Had it not been, then Liv would have never allowed her husband anywhere near her. His arms would have never been able to wrap neither in comfort around her nor their two children. She wouldn't have allowed him to, but she was in the dark about the sacrifice her daughter made for her to smile by his side.

Anger simmered in the heavens.

No one felt any pleasure in seeing such a cheerful person crumble into misery. It broke her son's heart and tore her daughter apart. They wanted nothing more than to bring solace to their mother, but how could they when the sentiment was shared? Their older sister's life hung in the balance.

Tears left all their eyes. Including Cassie's biggest monster of all. Luis Anas.

Somewhere deep in the recess of his consciousness eaten by guilt, but it paled at the thought he would no longer have a personal punching back. A sick man who even in moments as maddening as these thought of only everything he would lose. The moments where no one saw what he did to a poor little girl who sought for those around her to be happy.

Sorrow hung as a rainstorm around them. No comfort felt in each other's arms despite the deep craving their hearts had for it. Cassandra's present condition was an affliction for them all.

The tribulations and horrors that ripped her wings to shreds were now perhaps a secret they would never know about. Still, slivers of hope held prayers to a higher power in hopes it would all turn out alright.

Seconds became minutes and eventually hours; yet no updates on Cassie. They were all knives that kept twisting and turning. Bringing nothing but a deep-rooted agony.

Till the moment the doctor approached them at around six thirty in the morning, although Cassie had been brought in the previous day at four in the afternoon. A fact that had Olivia's nerves fried. Left her battered and desperate.

"How's my daughter?" Her words were frantic and urgent as she sprung to her feet from the couch she sat on. The doctor let out a sigh and inhaled deeply. His mind reeled as he held a tight grip on his emotions.

"She sustained multiple fractures and severe internal bleeding," Declan Alaniz proceeded to explain. "But she made it through the surgery," he adds, taking a beat. Relief flooded their hearts, only to be ripped away. "Unfortunately, she's fallen into a severe state of coma that we're unaware if she'll ever wake up from."

"Coma?" Liv breathed in grief. "How is this possible? My daughter was okay yesterday and now..."

"Mrs. Castillo, your daughter had a potent dose of opioids in her system that point to this having been a suicide attempt," Alaniz added, struggling to rein in his thoughts on their findings.

"That's not possible! My sister would never!" Luisa Anas bellows shell-shocked.

"She also sustained brain damage, but we won't know the severity until and *if* she wakes up," he concludes.

Sobs wrack out of Olivia and her son's arms wrap around her as they glare at the doctor for being the bearer of bad news. "How is this possible?" Luis Anas questions next to them both.

"Mrs. Castillo, past lesions were discovered on your daughter that does not match with the fall, which has aggravated her current delicate state," Declan states, void of emotion as he struggled to keep the contempt from his voice and gaze.

The signs were there, and he wasn't one to ignore them. If there was anything he hated with absolute certainty was those that harmed a child. And it was clear that Cassandra Castillo was someone's victim.

Confusion plagues Olivia as he heard his words.

The truth had surfaced to the surface, but there was no one to transcribe it. No one to tell it. It simply simmered there as people came up with their own assumptions of interpretation.

Luis would never speak of his sins. Becca's broken friendship with Cassie rendered her words unreliable to her family. While Cassie laid in a room with her soul barely tethered to her body in a limbo that had her closer to death than anything.

So the truth simply floated there as it always had, with the exception that this time it could be seen and heard.

"Past lesions?" Olivia questions dismayed, but upon seeing the contempt in the doctor's eyes, anger brought turmoil in its wake. "Are you implying that I abuse my daughter?"

She was met with silence.

"How dare you, when I've never raised my hand against any of my children!" Her shout reverberated through the waiting room.

"Anyone physically discipline your daughter? Her injuries are consistent and show them to have occurred gradually through a period of time," he inquires, giving her the benefit of the doubt. "She shows prior contusions that have yet to heal and were not retained from the fall."

"We've never laid a hand on her! Your reports have to be mistaken," Olivia claims in outrage. Far too easily forgetting the few instances she had witnessed, Luis put his hands on Cassie. But she had always spoken to him about it in private and it'd led to countless arguments between them.

Yet she was unaware that Luis did, in fact, use excessive violence when it came to Cassie. He had a tendency to smack her around mostly when it was just the two of them. Knowing and abusing her love for her family.

She'd written him out of it long ago.

Liv also remained clueless about the fact that Susan had physically assaulted her daughter a multitude of times. She was ignorant of the torture and bullying Jenine Squire and the entire school inflicted on Cassie. There was so much she didn't know.

Her words were lies and worse of all, she didn't know.

One, I can only hope Olivia discovers the truth and rights every wrong made against Cassandra. That she can grant her the justice she deserves, but beyond that, to slay her monsters.

She's always done right by her. Waving off a rich man's want to get rid of her baby and bringing her up on her own. Fighting to give her a better life. One day, even granting the man that had so easily been willing to get rid of her a second chance to be in his daughter's life.

Her only wrong had been bringing her husband into Cassie's life when she was two. Not seeing the damage he brought about in the child she so much loved. Regret will plague her when she discovers the truth.

"Then I suppose the truth shall come out," Declan relays

in a soft challenge. "The authorities have been notified and they shall be looking into it," he says, siding with the girl whose life he helped save.

"Authorities?" Luis Jr. questions confused.

"By law, we're required to report to the authorities when child abuse is suspected, as it is in Cassandra's case," he explains to him in a soft tone. He hoped to instill comfort in the boy in case he, too, was being abused so he could speak out. But he wasn't. Neither was Luisa.

No, their father only took to making their older sister pay for the broken plates in his life.

"Child abuse? I have already told you I've never laid a hand on any of my children!" Olivia exclaims in outrage as exhaustion takes a toll on her body.

"The authorities shall determine that," the doctor concludes. "Cassandra is currently in the ICU and, because of the severity of her state, no visitors are allowed. However, a family member may remain with her overnight," Declan informs her, looking at the clipboard in his hands.

As much as he hated it, by law he couldn't forbid them access to her until the abuse was proved. Still, a watchful eye would remain.

"The next few days will be detrimental to her condition, but I advise you to prepare for the worst. The outcome doesn't appear favorable," he admits solemnly before walking away. Hating that she could become another number of those who lost to the clutches of child abuse.

Cassie had once been promised to be saved when she broke the truth, but life had been unexpected and claimed lives instead.

And now it sought to claim that of an angel.

Olivia gazes heartbroken at the doctor. She knew the odds weren't great, but hearing the doctor say it made her fears a reality. More than ever, she prayed to God to grant her strength. To save her daughter.

She fell once more to the ground and her husband held her

through it all as if he weren't the cause of her grief. An hour later, Liv was swayed by her children and Luis to go home.

She didn't wish to leave Cassie's side. Her condition far too grave to leave her alone, but they presented a compelling argument. Rest and a shower so she could spend the night by her side. Till then, there was nothing to be done.

Luis drove them home, and between the three of them, they helped her out of the car, and by her asking up the stairs despite her bedroom being on the first floor. Her feet took her to her daughter's room, where she shut them out and locked the door behind her.

Her children begged her to open the door as she surveyed her daughter's room. An empty glass of water sat neatly on her daughter's desk, along with Cassie's phone and a stack of letters. She trekked over to her bed and took one of her stuffed animals into her arms, squeezing it as if it were her daughter and she was giving her an embrace.

Tears dove out of her as she tried to ease the pain. But nothing could make it go away. Her feet gave out and sobs echoed against the walls as her children begged her for the next hour to open the door. She never did, and they eventually gave up feeling helpless.

Cassie's phone buzzed on the desk and Olivia rose to her feet and made her way to it. Her hand brushing against the computer mouse by accident as she picked the device up, and opened it. Recorded notes with each of their names met her eyes. Sorrow drowned her once more.

A message popped up. Brad.

"Hey, I haven't heard from you since yesterday. Are you doing okay, Sie? Let's hang out later today."

Olivia cried at the words. Cassie's computer dinged once, then twice, and then once again as the screen now lit up. Liv's eyes trailed over to the monitor to find a multitude of screens lighting it up. Message after message appeared, and her gaze read over them.

"Die, Cassandra Castillo. No one wants you. You're a

waste of space!"

"Your father killed himself because he was ashamed of you. You're a killer."

"Come, please me. I'll even pay you ten bucks."

"Kill yourself, Cassie. Quit being a burden."

"You're a slut and whore. I hope you die."

Horror and shock paralyzed her. The hate and intensity of the messages shook her. Olivia's hand clasped over the mouse as she clicked and scrolled through the pages, seeing the filthy lies they'd spread about her daughter. The hateful pages where they slandered her good name down to the ones where she solicited men.

Page by page, she printed every single thing she found. Resolute to confront the school tomorrow, but today she sought to break. Shattered that she had missed the signs her daughter was being bullied.

The doctor's words come back to haunt her as her eyes glimpse at a fallen picture frame by her bed. Her feet moved toward it and she bent down to retrieve it from the floor. Only to catch sight of something she would have never guessed her daughter to own. A diary.

Consequences

Narrator

HER HANDS CLASP AROUND the journal hidden underneath Cassandra's bed as she picks it up off the floor. Her palm runs over the cover of the diary as she sits on the bed, wondering about the contents of the small notebook. It'd never crossed her mind that Cassie could possess such a thing, and it broke her that she did.

She had sought to write her struggles on paper instead of sharing them with her, her mother. Had she known, Liv would have done everything to help her. Maybe then Cassie wouldn't be in the hospital.

She broke as she looked at the words, but didn't register them. It felt foul to read her daughter's deepest thoughts. It was too much to bear.

Setting it to the side, she instead leaned down and picked up the photo that had originally caught her eye. One of Becca and Cassie smiling when they were eight. It reminded her of the betrayal. The one thing her daughter confided to her about.

Becks and Hugh sleeping together behind her back. Olivia has been outraged on her behalf, but her daughter had simply mourned the fact she had lost her best friend. She'd rid herself of every belonging or gift received by Hugh Squire, but everything about Becca remained.

Unable to look at it any further, Liv sets it down on the nightstand next to the bed where Cassandra kept it. Standing tall and proud.

The photo instilled her with courage as she rose from the bed and snatched both the diary and the printed copies off the printer. Cassie had been hurt, and she had to hold those responsible accountable.

She thanked God when she encountered no one on her way out of the house. Stopping only to write them a quick note and to grab her purse and husband's keys. She simply placed the journal and proof into her bag and drove off towards Cassandra's school.

Liv was a woman on a mission. It took her fifteen minutes to get there and five to burst into Principal Moore's office to demand explanations. No one could stop her.

"Mrs. Castillo, you simply cannot enter," Sanji, the director's secretary, scolded in a flush.

"I want to speak to my daughter's classmates regarding this," Olivia demands, pulling the printed pages out of her purse and slamming them onto the principal's desk.

The woman before her looked confused and sought to tell her something, but the look in Liv's eyes halted her words. Instead, she simply dismissed her secretary and took the pieces of paper with a sigh.

"What might this be?"

"Please read," Olivia coaxes in a strained voice.

Horror and shock overwhelm the woman as her eyes skim through the papers in her hands. A deep-rooted concern for the Cassandra Castillo grew as she read the hateful words and fear took hold when she came across the fake prostitution pages. Failure flooded her immediately.

Simply knowing a student was undergoing bullying at her school was inconceivable, but seeing the degree at to which she had been subjected... it was heartbreaking. Something she hadn't been witnessed to before.

How had it gone without her noticing?

She was speechless and angry.

Too little too late.

Cassie still lays in a hospital bed with one foot in the grave.

"Mrs. Castillo, I'm rendered mute to this horror and cannot apologize enough for the pain your daughter has been subjected to, but I assure you, I will personally deal with this issue."

Her words weren't good enough for Olivia. She needed something done now, and she wanted the ones responsible to face the consequences. Much like I do.

"My daughter attempted to take her life yesterday afternoon. You will do something now," Liv drawls out before taking a deep breath. "I've been recommended to look into making funeral arrangements because they don't think she'll make it. You won't hide this."

"I have no intention of hiding this," Moore assures her while searching for words of solace to give the woman before her. But none could be found. "Sanji, please convoke an assembly in the auditorium promptly. All staff and students present; no exceptions," she calls on her secretary through the intercom.

"I want the creators of these pages expelled," Olivia states the second the director hangs up her phone.

"Bullying is and will not be tolerated. Rest assured, they will face adequate punishment for their actions."

"The doctor informed me they found unhealed injuries on her persona... I've never laid a hand on any of my children and I was accused of child abuse," Liv shares with her. "But after reading all of this," she gestures to the pieces of paper she printed. "I'm getting the impression it happened here."

"Mrs. Castillo, accusations—"

"I will be taking this matter to the police," Olivia interrupts.

"I understand, but remember they are also children," Moore reminds her.

"If they can hurt my daughter with words and blows, then

they are old enough to face the consequences," Liv dismisses her. She had no mercy to give despite priding herself on her forgiving nature.

Cassie was being ripped away from her because of their fault. They were to blame, and she was going to make them pay for it.

"I'll be notifying parents," Moore affirms, knowing when a battle was lost.

"Dr. Moore, everyone has been convoked in the auditorium," Sanji announces, entering the office.

"Thank you," she replies, rising from her seat. "Mrs. Castillo, if you wouldn't mind accompanying me."

Liv nods and follows the woman out of her office and into the school auditorium. Everyone had to be made aware of Cassie's situation and those responsible had to be held accountable. School should be a safe space for learning and making friends; not the nightmare they created for Cassandra.

They were met with conversation flooding the vast space as students were wrapped in laughter, smiles, and chatter without a care in the world. Teachers spoke with one another in small groups, trying to assess the meaning of the assembly while overlooking the rowdy teenagers.

The sight broke Olivia's heart. Her daughter should have felt just as they did, but that was not the case. She lay on a bed with her life uncertain, while her tormentors remained unfazed.

Cassie could die, and they would live.

It wasn't fair.

"Everyone settle down," Paul Schroeder, one of the two vice principals of the school, orders the second he sees Principal Moore. Slowly, mouths clamped shut as their eyes settled over the two people approaching the stage.

Becca's heart instantly fell into dread. Turmoil had already plagued her upon not seeing Cassie in the morning. She knew her best friend never missed a day. The one time she hadn't come, had been when her father died and even that was brief. Seeing Olivia only made her alert that something was wrong.

"The room is yours," Paul Schroeder says, stepping away from the podium to stand next to Molly Hess, the second vice-president of the school.

Moore simply nods at him and steps behind the stand with Liv right there next to her. "It has been brought to my attention that bullying has been taking place at the school and that is simply unacceptable," Moore voices clearly through the microphone. Whispers run like wildfire across the rows.

Olivia's eyes scan the crowd below her for signs of any guilt or remorse, but there were none. Perhaps it was the distance between her and them. Nevertheless, she hoped to see something that showed them repenting. Nothing.

"Dr. Moore, no one here has bullied Cassie," Hugh speaks, taking a stand. "All we've done is tell her her truths. If she can't handle it, then that's her problem."

On his right, Jenine's judgmental eyes pierce his skin as she glowers at him in contempt. On his left, Becca gazed at him with nothing but horror. She'd been doing everything to stop the harassment and hearing the boy she loved had been part of it was heartbreaking. Her blindfold was falling, and Jenine hated her brother for it.

"Dr. Moore, I don't see what that stupid girl's problems have to do with my education, so what's the point of this assembly?" Fanilea stood up without a care.

"Sit down!" Jenine snapped at her; furious that her little follower had done something on her own once again. Admitting fault. Something Jenine Squire would never do.

"Quiet, the three of you if you don't wish to be suspended for three days," Moore warns, her patience null. "What was done to Cassandra Castillo was a cruelty! Bullying at this school is not condoned, and those involved with be facing the consequences of their actions."

"Cruelty? All we did is tell her the truth," another student rose in retaliation.

"A cruelty that led a young girl to attempt to take her own life," Moore corrects her. "Your parents are being notified, and the authorities will be getting involved."

"Authorities? What for? You just said she attempted to kill herself. How is any of that our fault!" Jenine demands, fearful Becca would find out. She would lose her best friend if it all came to be known.

"How can you live with yourself after putting her through hell? How dare you put your hands on my daughter and assault her?" Olivia questions dismayed. "She's the kindest person in existence, and if she dies, I will make sure you all end up in prison for murder."

"She pulled the trigger," someone chimes in.

"She did the world a favor!"

"Cassandra Castillo is a human being whose life hangs in the balance," Moore cuts through the uproar of students cheerful at such a horrid act.

"She's a bitch that ruins everything and has been sleeping with her stepfather," Fanilea argues.

"Fani, shut up!" Jenine snaps before Becca's mouth can even open.

"We didn't tell Cassie to kill herself!" Hugh screams, outraged.

"That's it. The three of you are suspended for two days," Moore retaliates.

"You have to be kidding me!"

"No one forced Cassandra to kill herself and you cannot punish us for her actions," Jenine spoke on behalf of her brother.

"Ms. Squire, make that a week of suspension," Dr. Moore corrects. "You may believe you played no part in her actions, but words cut just as deep Ms. Squire. Plenty of you wrote to her to end it all and quit breathing. For that and the aggressions made to her, the authorities shall be involved."

"No, you won't blame Cassie's entire suicide attempt on

them!" Becca shouts, breaking the silence and pleading for her best friend's forgiveness. "Your husband and the step-witch are as much to blame as these idiots!"

"What are you accusing my husband of, Becca? Being a loving father? How dare you speak of him after what you did to my daughter? Sleeping with her boyfriend..."

"So I made mistakes, but trust me, your husband is no saint. He's a monster that's been beating Cassie since he came into her life and moving up to rate the second her father appeared!" Becca transcribes the truth she knows, but her words fall on deaf ears. "Susan Pearce did nothing but beat and berate her, starving her when she could. Where were you when your daughter was drowning so you could smile?"

Her heart broke as tears flooded her eyes, and without a care, she stormed away. Cassie had tried to end her life once again, and she hadn't been there this time to stop her. She'd failed her.

"I'm going to be giving you the chance to come forward and perhaps be more lenient on your punishment for the harassment done to Cassandra Castillo. If no one comes forward, then there will be severe consequences for the entire school," Moore announces, bringing back the conversation to the subject at hand.

The auditorium went deathly silent.

"I created those pages to expose her as the skank she is," Fanilea boasts with pride. "What do you plan to do about it?"

"I helped everyone know the truth about who she truly was," Jenine admits, choosing her words carefully with a smile on her lips

"Consider yourselves expelled," Principal Moore conveys, choosing to make an example of them.

"Please, my daddy can pay for another school. One that is far better than this one," Jenine says viciously as she flips her hair over her shoulder.

Olivia's willpower broke, and her restraint snapped. She abandoned the stage and marched up to Jenine with blinded fury, striking her across the face.

"You should be ashamed of yourself. You broke my daughter and for that, I will make you pay. All of you. Because of you, my daughter chose she didn't want to live. So, listen to me, you wannabe Barbie. Your actions are unforgivable, and I will make you pay for them. I'll be sure you're the first to go down if she dies. You'll be the first one behind bars," Liv spits at her before abandoning the auditorium.

She took a few steps away from the cursed room before breaking down in the hallway while Becca did so in a bathroom nearby. Jenine's lack of empathy left her shaken. Her daughter didn't deserve any of it, and it killed her she had been a victim to some mean girl.

But it wasn't just Jenine who got to her. It was Becks as well. Olivia couldn't believe her husband to partake in any harmful act against Cassandra, but she's wrong. The dead know it well. There's no hiding the truth.

Her phone rang, and she answered, recognizing the number as Brad's.

"Hello?"

"Mrs. Castillo, I've been texting Cassie all night and haven't heard from her. I'm worried and have to know if she's alright?" He questioned with the urgency of someone who cared.

Liv sobbed, and Brad's concern only grew.

"Mrs. Castillo?"

"Cassie tried to kill herself yesterday," Olivia breathes out, shattering both of their hearts.

"Kill herself? How is she?"

"Doctors have little hope of her surviving. She's currently in a profound state of coma," she mutters in a strained voice.

"What hospital?"

"Angel Memorial Hospital."

"Who's her doctor?"

"I believe it was Alaniz, but I don't think it makes much of a difference," she replies, exhausted.

"Just hold on, Olivia, and make it right for Cassie. Have faith she'll make it through."

"I'm heading to the hospital right now. My siblings are both doctors at that same hospital," Brad conveys rushing to collect his things to go to Cassandra's side.

"They won't let you see her, dear. She's in ICU and visitors aren't allowed," Liv communicates with him.

"I have to try," he argues with certainty.

"Then I hope they let you. She could really use a friend," Olivia Castillo says before the line goes dead. "I'll make sure they pay, baby girl," she mumbles, leaving the school. She had one more stop to make before returning to Cassie's side. The police. They would all pay for her tears.

She would see it so.

Horrifying Truths

♥

Narrator

OLIVIA WENT STRAIGHT TO the police station and made a report regarding her daughter's aggressors. Shortly after, she was made to wait, and Becca's previous words came back to haunt her. Like they should.

And what she couldn't do before, she did at that moment. She pulled Cassie's diary out of her purse and read the thoughts her daughter wrote on paper to never escape. Slowly they registered and tears welled up in her eyes.

Every word was a jab to her heart. Every one of them proved Becca's words true. Her credibility was void to her, but Cassie's?

They would always hold. She meant everything to her.

There was no mistaking Cassandra's handwriting, or the pain she felt as she bled it onto the paper.

Luis Anas, her husband of nearly fifteen years, had raped her daughter. Confusion mixed with her grief as questions plagued her.

How could she have missed it? How could she not have noticed? How could she have let her daughter down?

Cassie's best friend, Becca Jones, was right; she'd failed her daughter. But she wasn't the only one. Everyone did. Now Cassie struggled to keep breathing.

She, along with everyone else, had been blind to the agony and weight over Cassandra's shoulders. Olivia's heart became torn, and her loyalty was split for a fraction of a second. She doubted her own daughter's words, and she hated herself for that brief moment of doubt.

Her faithfulness to her husband begged her to keep quiet. The words Cassie referred to the horrid acts he committed against her had her drowning. But in the end, her love for Cassie won.

She would never lie. Little details she had seen before and brushed off, as nothing now made perfect sense. Luis Anas was a monster.

He hurt Cassandra and for that; he had to pay. No matter how much it hurt. She had to face her husband's horrifying truths and put him behind bars.

Wasting no time, she took advantage of her surroundings and made another report. This time against the man that stood by her for years.

Clearly, it had been at a cost far too high for the innocent.

Liv couldn't let him hurt other children or the two they shared. Once an abuser, forever one. She wouldn't turn a blind eye.

Cassie was petrified of him, leading to her falling off a balcony.

The blame had to fall onto those responsible. Her husband was clearly one of them. It was heartbreaking to admit her husband's raping of her led to Cassie being bullied by her peers.

It was worse to see selfish people had twisted her daughter's truth and made it into a horrid narrative. But knowing the only reason that man had only ever been attentive with them was his way of repenting and keeping her daughter quiet nearly killed her.

Luis Anas was hiding dark secrets for which she would ruin him. He would really come to regret laying his dirty hands on her. He was meant to love and protect her, but instead, he broke her daughter.

He had chosen to become her father long ago and not sharing blood did not excuse his abusive behavior.

"Mrs. Castillo, are you certain of this?" The police officer questions her as she signs the police report.

"He touched my little girl. He needs to pay. I cannot let that go," she asserts, handing him the diary in a world of agony.

"You've raised a report against Jenine Squire and your husband. Anyone else you wish to file charges against?" He questions and she shakes her head.

"No, but I give you access to her computer and diary," Olivia offers. "I failed her, didn't I?"

He sighs and shakes his head. "In cases such as these, the abuser is someone the child knows, and they're groomed to keep silent. The victims get too good at lying and hiding it. Screaming into the silence, hoping someone notices it."

"And I never did."

"We'll be looking further into it and bring them all to justice," he assures her out of words of wisdom.

"Oh god, I left that man with my children before leaving the house," she says remembering his whereabouts. "I have to get home."

"We'll have a few officers accompany you to take your husband into custody."

Liv nods, and in brief minutes they're pulling up to her house. A patrol car behind her own, granting her a moment of comfort. Grief floods her as she abandons the car and enters the house.

It hits her that after today she'll lose her husband. Hurt beats through her as she races inside to meet Luis and her two children.

Questions plague her at their sight.

Were they enduring the same hell that Cassie was? Had he done to them what he did to her? Or were they always safe because they shared his blood?

"Dear, you're back," he greets her as she embraces and

holds her children tight. He takes a step toward her, but she recoils with them at the sight. Confusion marks on his face.

"Get away from my children," she yells at him. Fury burned within her at the acts he committed against Cassie. He became her worst nightmare when he had elected to be her father.

"Sweetheart, what's wrong?" Luis questions her, dismayed. Feigning as if he had no clue of the pain he had inflicted on Cassie.

"How could you hurt her in such a way? She was your daughter from the moment we got together. You chose to be her father! You raised her and raped her," she screams while shielding her kids.

His eyes reflect disbelief, but she was done believing the charade. Cassie meant more than having a companion in life. Her children outweighed the love she felt for him. She could get over him in time, but never over losing her children.

"What in the world are you talking about? I would never hurt Cassandra, Olivia!" He defends. "I love her, she's my daughter," he says calmly, but even the words reflect the lie they are.

Liv releases her son and daughter only to march to him and slap their father across the face once. Then twice. Still, she felt no relief.

"Don't bother lying, it won't help you anyway," she drawls as the police officers enter the house and make their presence known. "I hope you rot in jail," she spits, retreating to her children and embracing them with her arms as they, too, cried.

"Olivia, please, I would never hurt her," he pleads, as the officers slap the cuffs on and lock them tight. Liv shakes her head and strokes her children's heads.

He'd ruined Cassie, and she wouldn't let him harm their kids any further.

A smile makes its way onto my face at the sight of Olivia choosing our daughter and making it right. She found the truth and struck down at every one of her demons like the momma bear she's always been.

"You won't hurt anyone else where you're going," she mumbles quietly as they walk him out to their car. "You ruined this family, Luis."

He would pay for his wrongs and the pain he brought. Still, it didn't feel like enough. Cassie's state was unwavering, a limbo without answers. She'd taken matters into her own hands and it was destroying everyone that truly knew her.

Even in death, the guilt written over Olivia's face is palpable. She blamed herself for everything. She blamed her ignorance and if Cassie dies, there is no doubt in my mind that she'll believe the blood on her hands.

"I might be her guardian angel from heaven, but you, Olivia, are hers on Earth."

Becca

The air in the auditorium was asphyxiating. Cassie tried to kill herself, and I wasn't there. There's no one to blame but me. I broke the vault.

I let her secrets out and despite my trying so I've been unable to set things right. Every rumor I get Jenine to quiet down, it all starts like wildfire all over again. My best friend paid the price because I let popularity blind me.

I'm a terrible human being.

I witnessed so many acts against her, but did nothing in front of anyone. No, I helped from the dark because I was afraid to lose what I gained. But now it's clearer than ever that I was wrong.

I betrayed my best friend, and now she's dying.

Pain overwhelms me at the thought that I chose Jeni over her. It's only natural Cassie succumbed to so much pain. I should have reached out. Done more.

Tears and sobs resonate over the bathroom walls as I break down, letting my mask of popularity slip. None of it means anything without the one that has always been there for me. It's only a reminder that it was the reason for my best friend's downfall.

What would have happened had I been honest with her and left all of this? Had I never given her my back?

"Becky, what was that?" Jeni questions me from behind, and I raise my head to meet her eyes through the mirror. "Everything you told that woman, what was that? You were meant to have Fani's back! It's what friends do!"

"The truth, Jenine. I told her the truth, you and I know. Cassie has never once slept with her stepfather. He's raped her time and time again. I wasn't going to idly stand by and let her degrade her with lies!" I exclaim in bubbling rage.

"Why do you keep taking that bitch's side?" Fanilea screams.

"Quit calling her that! Cassie is an angel. Better than all the people in this world combined. She's dying because of all of us. Because I broke her silence and chose something as superficial as popularity over her."

"Popularity is not superficial. It's everything, Becky. Really, how have you not got that by now?"

"No one cares for the truth Becky, so long as Cassie remains destroyed," Fani retaliates, siding with Jeni like always.

"I've just been expelled and her mother is taking this to the police as if it were my fault when I've done nothing but help you," Jeni groans, frustrated.

"I care! You've done little to help her. Hell, I'm beginning to think, Jeni, that it was all your doing. Everyone always listens to you and this has yet to blow over. My best friend is dying because I trusted you."

"I'm your best friend Becky," Jeni corrects me.

"No, she is, and I'll never forgive myself for the part I played in ruining an innocent soul who may now die because of our fault."

"Yet you slept with her boyfriend and told me all her secrets to destroy her," Jenine snaps with her eyes glimmering with unshed tears.

"I knew you were too good to be true, Jeni. You have no idea how much I regret trusting you."

"Quit defending that whore!" Fanilea spits in my direction, and I roll my eyes at her. "We just got rid of her, and she's already causing mayhem. Why couldn't she die properly?"

I jump back onto the sink as her arrogance speaks. Horror drowning my veins as I dread the words to come out of her mouth. Fanilea is a follower, but she's also dangerous. I've always known that. I can't underestimate her.

"I made mistakes but refuse to take the sole blame for Cassie's suicide attempt," I snap at her, feigning an indifference I don't feel.

"Fani, shut up," Jeni warns her.

"I push her off her damn balcony and she's already breaking us all apart," Fani confesses with irritation in the undertones of her voice.

My heart stops.

"You pushed her?"

"So she could pay for her crimes and leave Jeni alone. Really, it's something you should have done sooner," she adds. "She's a liar Becky. Why are you defending her?"

"Did you know about this?" I ask Jeni with a broken voice.

"Please Jeni, knows. She was there with me," Fani reveals, and my trust in Jenine breaks. She lied and used me.

"I did not tell you to kill her! We were there to teach her a lesson. Fani simply got carried away."

"How can you say it so calmly?" I breathe out in shock.

"She rid me of a trouble. Did the right thing, above all," Jeni defends the psycho who follows her like a sick puppy. "I have no intention of betraying one of my closest friends for a whore."

They tried to kill Cassie. There's more to the story that

Olivia Castillo knows and told. Jeni and Fanilea pushed her. I betrayed her once more.

I once promised to do right by Cassie once more, but I failed. Now I won't be making that same mistake. She deserves better from me.

The two people I've called friends for the last few weeks will not get away with this.

Without another word, I abandon the bathroom and find my way to the place that will hold them accountable. The very one Olivia mentioned. The police.

"Hello, I want to report an attempted murder," I announce the second I arrive, gaining immediate attention. Fani and Jeni will pay even if I lose them. They were never Cassie anyway.

Real friends don't use you; they stand with you through thick and thin.

Love?

Brad

I DIDN'T WANT TO believe it, but Cassie's mom wouldn't lie over something as delicate as her life. The girl I like attempted to take her own life. My new friend chose death over...

I knew something was wrong and going on, but thought she would tell me with time. Now I see I should have pushed instead of waiting. Maybe then I could have helped her and she wouldn't have done this.

Hard to believe someone so sweet and vulnerable would turn to something as permanent as this. She bore a look of sadness, but she always had a smile on her lips that disarmed anyone. I should have done more for her.

She's become easily my best friend ever since I saved her from that car, who didn't even bother to stop and make sure she was okay. Her recruiting to this instead of me hurts. I would have been there for her and done everything I could to help her and not simply because of the connection I feel with her.

It's more than that.

Could this be because of her boyfriend and best friend's betrayal? I wanted nothing more than to teach the guy a lesson for making her cry. I'd felt an immeasurable anger for something that hadn't even happened to me. I'd wanted to wash her pain and hurt away.

I wish I would have been able to. Maybe that's what drove her to this. Their fooling around with one another behind her back.

Love doesn't die overnight, clearly. Me taking her out to eat after and us simply laughing all day as we spent our day at the mall didn't heal the broken heart he left behind.

How he got a hold of an angel and let her go; I will never know.

That's what Cassie is, an angel that carried the weight of the world on her shoulders. Now it makes sense that she always avoided the simple questions regarding if she was okay. I regret accepting her *"I'm fine"* response when she wasn't.

I was her friend, and I failed her.

My heart feels heavy as I race through the hospital hallways in search of Deck, hoping to find him in his office. Stopping for nothing or no one, even as I stumble over my own feet. I slam his office door open to find him in a compromising position with a coworker.

I definitely did not need to see that. Now it's carved into my brain forever, but for Cassie, I'll live with it.

His gaze fixates on me, annoyed the second I clear my throat and announce my presence. The woman pushes him off and scurries away, fixing her own clothing. She glances briefly at me before darting out of the office without a single word.

"You just interrupted my—"

"Don't finish that sentence and worry about your own needs later," I cut him off, not needing any of the details. "I need your help."

"What's wrong?" His question bleeds with concern, and I sigh, running my fingers through my hair. "How can I help?"

"Is Cassandra Castillo one of your patients?"

"Brad, what is this about?"

"I need to know if you're her doctor," I plead with him. "Her mother said her doctor's surname was Alaniz and if it's not you, then it's Pia, or tell me who is treating her."

"Why?"

"She's my friend. Now answer my question," I beg him. "Is it you?"

"Cassandra Castillo is both Pia, and I's patient," he concedes, and I breathe in relief.

I know both he and Pia will do everything to keep her breathing. They're good at what they do. I've seen it.

"Declan, I need to see her," I petition and he shakes his head at me, breaking my heart.

"Brandon, she's in the ICU," he says solemnly. "Authorized personnel only. No visitors and only a family member can stay overnight with her."

"Please..."

He sighs. "Don't look at me like that," he requests, but soon tears are running down my cheeks and he sighs. I haven't cried since our parents passed away.

"Let me see her," I plead once more. I'm not above it to see her. I'll do anything to see Cassie right now.

"Declan, the authorities are here to question you over Cassandra Castillo's condition," Pia says, coming into the office and he pulls his gaze away from me and towards our sister. "Brad."

"Pia, please, let me see Cassie," I beg of her, a sob rippling out of me. Her arms are quick to envelop me as I break down at the thought of losing her.

"He's friends with Cassandra Castillo," Declan supplies.

"Tell me she's going to live," I implore to them both. Sighs meet my ears.

"The next few hours are critical, but there's little hope she'll make it," Pia confesses to me in a soft voice, much like the one our mother used before her death.

"I need her to live. You have to do everything you can," I beseech them.

"We will," Declan assures me. "But like I told her mother, you need to be prepared for the worst little brother."

"Declan, shut up and go see the police officers waiting for you in the waiting room," Pia snaps at him. He sighs and leaves his office without another word.

"Why does he need to talk to them?"

"We suspect Cassie is the victim of severe child abuse, and by law we are mandated to report it to the authorities," she conveys, much more open about it than my brother was. "How do you know her?"

"She's the girl I've been seeing lately."

"Is she the one you saved?" She asks and I nod.

"Please, I need to see her," I press, hoping my sister takes pity on me.

A sigh escapes her. "I really shouldn't be doing this, but I can tell she means a lot to you, so just this once," she cedes. "Follow me."

She guides us out of Deck's office and towards wherever Cassie is. A mixture of emotions muddles my mind as I follow Pia through a maze of hallways. People glance occasionally in our direction and it takes me a second to realize why.

My cheeks remain wet with tears that continue to unapologetically fall. It's not common to see a guy display his emotions so openly. Sad, really, that they wish to stereotype me into a box to keep quiet.

Thankfully, my parents believed in none of it and I was told from the start I never had to hide how I feel. It is my right to be entitled to my feelings and they will forever be valid no matter what anyone says. I'm no less of a person because I wear my heart on my sleeve, if anything it makes me better.

"Did you know if she was being hurt by someone at home?"

"She never mentioned anything," I answer Pia. "What makes you believe she's a victim of child abuse?"

"She has unhealed lesions that never got proper medical treatment. Some recent and others long ago," my sister explains.

"Is it that bad?"

Pia remains silent but nods at me in admission.

"I'm hoping your visit can aid in her healing," she admits as we come to a stop at a door. Nerves eat at me as she pulls on the handle, but stops. "Be ready. She has machines helping her breathe and is in a profound state of coma. Don't be frightened."

Worry trickles down my spine as she opens the door and gestures for me to go inside. A frog gets caught in my throat as I take a step forward and I stop at the doorway as shock paralyzes me.

A few feet before me, Cassie lies so fragile and beaten on a bed. Bandages over her small frame, and bruises marking the small patches of skin visible. She lay there lifelessly connected to tubes. The sight alone broke my heart.

I force my legs to move and enter the room, my breath abandoning me with every step I take. Inches away from the bed, I place my hand over hers gently to avoid hurting her as I kiss her forehead lightly. My fingers thread her hair to remind myself she's still here.

My lips brush against her cheek, by the corner of her lips, and I feel terrible. I've been meaning to kiss her for so long and now I may never get the chance. I want her to be awake so I may get the chance to explore the connection between us.

"I can't believe I'm seeing you like this," I confess. "You look so weak and fragile, but you're the strongest person I know. I hate seeing you like this. I don't want you to die..."

My words get lost as a sob escapes me. Pia was right she looks different. It's hitting me that the girl that has made herself a special place in my heart might die. These might be her last moments on Earth.

"Please, Cassie. If you can hear me, fight. I need you to fight. For me... for you... for your mom... for your siblings... You're special and loved. You matter so much to us and we need you. Don't leave us yet."

A whimper leaves me as my vision blurs at the sound of the beeps on the machine. Cassie has to live. I can't lose her.

"I care about you... I love you, Cassie. You have to wake up so I can tell you face to face," I weep, breaking down.

Wait, did I just say I love her?

It can't be. She and I have only known each other for a short time. Love doesn't come to be that fast, does it?

Her sweet smile comes to mind, and my heart skips a beat at the thought.

I love her.

What if she hurts me as Prim did? What if she never wakes up? Worse, what happens if she dies?

Cassie

A smile lights up my face as I look at my surroundings. Nature envelops me in its peace and I'm free from pain. Happiness flowers in my chest, knowing I have nothing to fear.

I never want to leave.

It's everything I've ever dreamed of having. I'm living a beautiful and magical dream. One I never want to wake from.

Death was the right choice.

"I can't believe I'm seeing you like this," Brad's voice echoes. "You look so weak and fragile, but you're the strongest person I know. I hate seeing you like this. I don't want you to die..."

My eyes dart everywhere in search of him, but he's not here. I'm alone.

Where is his voice coming from then?

"Please, Cassie. If you can hear me, fight. I need you to fight. For me... for you... for your mom... for your siblings...

You're special and loved. You matter so much to us and we need you. Don't leave us yet."

Wait, fight? Does that mean I'm not dead? I have to be.

Dread creeps up my spine as I retreat into the paradise I'm in. No, I can wait for death to find me here. I refuse to go back.

"I care about you... I love you, Cassie. You have to wake up so I can tell you face to face," his voice cracks as cries ripple through and thunderstorms resound in the sky above me.

My head shakes by its own volition as I walk away from him. I don't want to go back to a world of pain where I'm everyone's punching bag.

No. Resolution fills me as I drown his voice out and prance further into my little oasis, where I'm its only resident. No one to hurt me. It's perfect.

I'm sorry, Brad, but I'm not going back for anyone. Not you or my family. You'll all be okay without me. I rather be dead than alive. There's no pain in the beyond. I'm far too happy to leave.

"Cassie, please, it kills us to see you this way."

My head shakes once more as I hum an old poem titled *Broken* that I scribbled on a page long ago.

"I thought I could protect them from the monster in the shadows, but I was wrong. I thought if I did what he said then he wouldn't harm my family. I thought I could sacrifice myself and come out unharmed. Again, I was wrong.

The monster broke me like no one else had before.

He tore me into pieces. He broke every fiber of strength I had. He took my purity and danced with joy as he did. He didn't think twice about hurting me; breaking me.

For I was not his daughter, and this was his revenge for raising me as such. I thought I could escape his class of destruction, but I didn't make it out in time.

I screamed for help, but my screams were drowned by the darkness in him. My screams were silent, but I thought someone would notice. No one did, and it became a routine for me.

I shattered against the ground and broke into a million pieces, and no one seemed to care or notice. I tried to escape, but there was none. Now my ruins lie around and I won't ever be the same. I'm broken beyond anyone's repair."

The poem cements my resolution to stay. It's my truth, and not even Brad could fix or heal my wounds. I'm shattered and I can't even find or know where all the pieces are. I no longer believe in happy endings; they don't exist, at least not for me. Here, I'm happy and that's good enough for me.

I walk inside my little cottage and close the door without glancing back. I'll remain in my dream world until I leave this world for good. If God exists, then he owes me that much.

:(Please Help Me :(

♥

Can anybody hear me?
Has anyone even heard my pleads?
Why won't anyone help me?
I have called out about a million times
I am silently calling out for help
I am desperate to be saved
Have you heard my silent pleads in the nights?
Does anybody even care about me?
Why am I still alive in this cruel world?
Time stands still as my tears drop
And all I can seem to wish is death
When will I be free from this pain?
I feel as if there is nothing less of me
I'm on the ground bleeding and in pain
No one in sight to help me up
I feel alone and in the dark
When will I find the light?
When will this stop?
When will I be free?
No one helps me
I just wish to be dead
I'm alone in the stone-cold ground
Help me from the other side

¿FRIENDS?

Please I beg you
I'm in pain and no one seems to care
In times like this, I wish to be dead
Death seems the answer
I've tried to call for help a 1,000 times
No one has heard my pleas
My only way out is death
I'm tired of feeling pain
Of being used and beaten every day
Of being hurt every day, hour, minute
They laugh as I bleed and cry for help
Why are they so cruel to me?
Why do they break me?
Why do they take everything I have?
Why do they break everything I am?
Why oh why can't this hell go away?
Why can't I stop Rolling in the deep?
Help me oh please
Why won't anyone help me?
The sky falls down on me every day
People watch but ignore me
I'm broken
And break down more by day
Why do they do this to me?
Is this ever going to end?
I just want this to end?
People wonder but don't ask
Why can't this end?
Won't anybody help me?
Please help me
Won't anybody help me?
I'm in pain
Please help me
Won't you help me?

Brave

Narrator

TIME PASSED QUICKER THAN anyone would have liked. Everything seemed to be frozen when it came to Cassie's condition. There were no improvements or deterioration. Doctors were becoming alarmed by the second.

There was no sign at all that she was there.

By day she showed no signs of brain activity and they feared her gone.

"Mrs. Castillo, it might be time to let go and look into alternative routes, such as organ donation. There has been no change, nor has there been any sign of brain activity. We must face the facts, your daughter will never wake up," Declan attempts to reason with Olivia.

She simply shakes her head and brushes him off as her eyes land on her daughter's frail form on the bed.

She couldn't let her die. Her heart wouldn't allow her to turn the machines off. She harbored the hope that a miracle would occur and Cassie would beat the odds. She would wake up and be okay.

It didn't matter that days slowly turned into weeks and drifted into months. Liv shut down every attempt made to pull the plug on Cassandra. She had faith God would give her her daughter back. But as the clock ticked forward, her faith wavered and despair set in.

Regardless, she was unable to give up on Cassie. Despite the pain, it brought all of them. With the only highlight being Cass's demons coming forth to meet justice.

Her biggest monster, Luis Anas, was sentenced to over thirty-seven years in prison without the chance of parole for the pain he inflicted on Cassie. His children wept that day at the loss of their father while their mother held them. Her heart broken as much as theirs.

Jenine and Fanilea were sentenced to twenty years behind bars for the transgressions committed against Cassandra, along with their attempted murder. Apparently, the fact Cassie had chosen to take her own life first weighed heavily on the jury and diminished the crime itself in their eyes.

But it could have also been because of the expensive lawyer assigned to bail them out. Although even he couldn't save her from the punishment of her crime. Becca's testimony had made certain of that. Still, neither one of Jenine's parents showed to court, unlike her brother, who never missed a hearing.

Soon, word spread about Cassandra Castillo, the girl who underwent a great deal of pain in the shadows. The media's attention was attracted, but her family didn't care. Not even as they spoke of Cassie's strength and resilience to the abuse she suffered.

Their spotlight came too late onto the truth. Her life now remained confined to a bed. Forever in a state of uncertainty.

Her body healed slowly, with the casts for her broken bones eventually being removed. But her state remained the same, and it broke the hospital's staff's heart to see her family trading days staying with her. Even Brad. None of them losing hope that she would wake up.

Olivia blamed herself for being blind to Cassie's torment, but then I'm to blame as well. I never noticed the hits or the agony shining so clearly in our daughter's eyes. Now I'm a spectator guarding over her.

A smile graced my lips when Olivia the day Luis Anas was served with divorce papers in prison where the other inmates didn't take too kindly to his vicious acts. Paying him the same mercy he had with Cassie.

They all kept her informed of events, but she was far too gone to hear them. They decorated her room and kept her company even as they moved her from the ICU. Every time they were with her, pleas would slip past their lips for her to wake, but she never did.

Slowly, hope chipped away at their fragmented soul.

Even the removal of the tool helping her breathe didn't snap her eyes open. Time was wearing them all down and having them age faster.

Stress ate at them all.

Including Becca, who had taken to visiting Cassie and leaving popularity behind. Realizing even if late that none of that was important. Leaving Hugh when she came to realize the flaws he held.

She'd won them all over in a heartbeat. The only regrets she wore were the ones where she wasn't by her best friend's side when she most needed her. But she vowed to make it right and do right by her. Now till the day they died.

Becks was certain of it. This time, she would choose friendship above all else. It's the hardest treasure to find. And Cassie was every bit of gold there was.

Cassie

Their voices are faint whispers begging for my return, but I block them out. They interrupt the peace I created for myself. Their words only make me feel like a coward, but I'm tired of being strong.

I've been so my whole life, so why can't they let me go?

If only they could all be silenced like I was and death would finally grace me with its presence and take me away.

Brad hasn't spoken to me of love ever since his first declaration. It brings me glee that he hasn't, otherwise, I would have caved and gone back.

I'm not ready to open my eyes or face the pain that comes with it. I've tried to heal my heart and soul in paradise, but I've failed.

There is no repair. There is no healing me. I'm far too broken.

I'm nothing but a burden. I'm tired of their happiness resting on my shoulders. I simply want to be left alone so I won't hurt anymore. Nothing but their words can haunt me here. I'm safe from the monsters, so why do they insist on dragging me back?

Narrator

After much insistence by all, Declan and Pia allowed them all to be in Cassie's room at once. By now, there wasn't much that they wouldn't dare try to see if a miracle occurred. It was killing them both to see their baby brother so devastated.

Medically speaking, there was no reason for her to remain in a coma. Her lesions had healed, and if she still hadn't, then it meant she was gone. But she was and is still in there.

They both watched with heavy hearts as they all chatted with Cassie for hours, only for her eyes to remain closed. Not even a stir that alerted them to her being there. Every one of them shattered a little more at it.

They expressed their goodbyes and headed to the door, exhaustion weighing heavily on them.

Her eyes shot open with anguish and pain plaguing them like the deathly disease they were. Becca's eyes met hers first, and a gasp escaped her. She stood frozen as her gaze locked onto her best friend's.

Heads slowly turned, and their souls found solace in seeing her awake. Joy rushed sloshed through their veins at the sight of her open eyes. It was everything they'd wanted.

But Cassie was terrified. Mortified. Of the monster and the demons. Completely unaware that her tormentors were paying for their crimes. They could no longer hurt her, and yet terror broke through her veins.

The idea of seeing Becca with Hugo was barely tolerable. It killed her to know *he* was far more important to Becks than she was. She'd trusted them and they'd driven a knife to her spine. But she only cared for the one her best friend had wielded. It was the only one that hurt.

There was no one to protect her from her stepfather. In her eyes I was gone, a truth that hurt her as much as it did me. She no longer had an escape plan that would immediately get her away from the monster.

Fear clamped her lips silent with tar. Refusing to part open when they'd been shown her word and pain meant nothing. If push came to shove, she was certain they would believe him. He'd created the perfect image, and she was simply the rebellious stepchild who didn't listen.

Even death had rejected her once.

The memories were drowning her as much as her emotions. Her insides were in turmoil as silent tears burst from her eyes and soon they turned into uncontrollable sobs. She couldn't go back to live with that *man*, and she couldn't return to school. Both were hell.

Insults, lies, manipulation. Blows, hits, blood. They all claimed something from her and she had nothing to give.

She wouldn't go back.

Everyone crowded around her, embracing her in the biggest and most affectionate hug, while her eyes were in search of another way to get death to come for her. Despair and anxiety were eating at her. Her eyes landed on the scissors near her bed that had been used to add further decorations to her room.

Cassie reached for them and hid them, waiting for them to leave so she could embrace the goodbye she wanted. Rid the world of the mistake it made by bringing her to life.

"Everyone please, step outside so we may examine her," Pia urges as Declan helps her usher everyone out of the room.

Fearing they would find her scissors and steal them away, Cassie took a chance. She used the distraction to pull the sharp object out and brought it to her wrists to slash through it. Certain that death would take her this time around.

Brad's eyes registered her actions before the metal could break through her flesh. He leaped into action and pushed them away from her wrist as he struggled to take them away from her grip. "Cassie don't!"

"No, give them back! I can't go back to hell, I just can't," she pleaded as the scissors fell to the floor. Her body twisted as she tried to retrieve them, but he fought against her.

"Cassie, calm down please," Liv pleads with our daughter, hoping she'll hear her, but deaf ears hear nothing. Cassandra fights him with all her might and they're forced to pin her to the bed as Pia applies a sedative that reacts instantly.

Her body slacks as it falls back into slumber.

"Why did she react that way?" Olivia asks both the medics before her as they close Cassie's hospital door behind them after escorting them to the hallway.

"It's clear she bears deep scars on the events that led her to take her own life, and she's yet to register she's safe. In her mind, she's going to have to face those who hurt her. For her it's as if no time has passed," Pia explains.

"We'll be contacting our psych ward and restraining her to the bed so she won't be able to attempt it again," Declan supplies.

"I've ruined my daughter's life," Olivia sobs as her children embrace her in a tight hug.

"For the time being, we're denying visitors until after Cassie has been seen by someone from the psych ward. They'll know how to best proceed," Pia declares. They all simply nodded. If it was what Cassie needed, then they would do it.

Cassie

My eyes flutter open at the soft sound of beeps. It takes me a minute to adjust to the lighting of the room and for me to get familiarized with my surroundings. Everything crashes onto me at once and the machine beeps louder and faster.

I pull at the cables and sit up on the bed.

Why am I alive? I want to be dead!

My hands pull the covers away as I attempt to scurry away from the bed, but my legs remain unmoving. What's going on? Anxiety cripples me as it has so many times before and I pull at them to swing them over to the side.

I'm alone in this room, but I know that won't last long. This place might be decorated with keepsakes I hold dear to my heart, but it's nothing more than a vacant black hole pulling me towards a life of pain I don't want.

No one else seems to care what I wish for. They want me to live. For what?

Shaking my head, I push myself off the bed and put my entire weight onto my feet, but they remain still when I propel them to move forward. Instead, they wobble meekly before I fall face first onto the floor.

Pain ripples through me as I scan for a permanent exit and my eyes land on the open window at the far end side of my room. The sound of passing cars meets my ears as a building comes into perspective. I'm not on the first floor of this hospital.

Having no choice but to crawl, I use my arms to drag myself across the room.

I'm not living another day in a world of pain. Less in a wheelchair. The monster will only hurt me more than he already does. I will not be at his mercy any longer, or Jenine's. No, I'll be joining my dad in death.

Tears well up in my eyes as I pull myself up onto the window and swing one leg after the other over it. My gaze is transfixed on the cars down below as I prepare myself to take the leap. Debating for one second if this is truly what I want.

My thoughts come to a halt as the door opens and I whip my head to see who it is. Two people. A woman and a man. One in a lab coat while the other wore simple yellow scrubs with restraints in his hands.

"How—"

Her words go mute as she fixates on the fact I'm no longer in bed and instead over the ledge of the window, ready to jump.

"Stay back!" I scream when the man takes a step forward. My grip holding on tight to the edges of the window.

"Cassie, you don't want to do that. Please don't!" She beseeches me but I shake my head the second she takes a step closer, pushing my body weight further out the window.

"Stay back! Stay back or I'll jump," I warn her at her fourth step and she stops, worry etched onto her face.

"Cassie, please, let's get you down from there. Let's talk about this. Things aren't as you imagine them to be."

"I can't go back to that hell," I breathe, shifting my gaze once more to the distance between me and the ground. It'll hurt, but it'll be brief. I can do it right this one time. I know it.

"No one is going to take you back to that hell. Your tormentors are in jail, you're safe," she pleads with me, but I know better. She's lying, and lies don't work for me. I refuse to listen to them.

"Tell them I'm sorry, but I can't," I whisper in tears before pushing myself off the ledge.

"Cassie! No!" she screams, but it's too late. I'm already falling and welcoming death with open arms. It's too late for me. I can't be saved. Only be taken by death to a genuine life free of pain.

Fallen Angel

♥

Cassie

THE WIND HITS MY skin with force as I descend onto the ground. Regret and fear fleet as I'm overwhelmed with peace and glee at the thought of being free of my hell. My demons will be left behind and breathing won't hurt anymore. I'll be with my dad once more.

The tears I spilled will be forgotten with time as I'll fade to be one more number of children lost to the hands of child abuse, bullying, and suicide. Everyone will forget me with time. Pretty withered roses always are.

Nothing merited me staying and continue the fight simply to keep breathing. I've drowned enough for those I love to be happy. Now it's my turn.

I'm done with the pain. No one cares anyway. They all failed me. I refuse to live in a world where I'm nothing but a mistake paying for everyone's broken plates.

My body meets the hard ground and shatters at impact. Every bone is crushed and unmeasurable agony floods my veins, but it's brief. My lungs collapse on themselves and my gasps for oxygen are short and null. Life slips from me as death finally embraces me into its grasp.

Eyes flit over to my wrangled broken body as gasps overfill the growing crowd. A high pitch scream filters through my conscious mind before I'm nothing more than a corpse. *"I'm sorry."*

My heart beats for the last time and I choke on the blood. Air abandons me and my soul lifts from the broken mess. Goodbye cruel world.

My gaze is pulled in by Brad, who stands next to my siblings, looking at my destroyed body. My mother's cries ripple in the air, and regret meets me for a second.

No one can touch me now. Not my demons or those I love. I can't be hurt, but those I love now hurt. I was okay with it. But seeing her grief over my death could easily kill me if I still breathed. I calculated wrong.

A hand clasps over my shoulder and, as I turn to face its owner, meeting sweet, tender eyes. Tears of joy fill my eyes as I leap into his embrace. The pain melted away into overwhelming happiness as his warmth seeps into my battered soul.

Everything clicks as my dad holds me in his arms. I came through on my promise. Becoming a fallen angel to look over those who undergo the same pain I did without being able to do anything.

Narrator

Pia Alaniz lept hoping to catch Cassandra Castillo's hand, but she was too late. Cassie was already falling with a smile on her lips at the thought of no pain. While the doctor agonized over her death and not being able to save her.

She watched in horror as her body shattered against the ground and the life leave her russet brown eyes. There was truly no doubt this time that Cassandra Castillo was truly gone this time. Becoming one more victim that people would mourn after when they did nothing to help her in time.

She'd been hurt one too many times. The tinted glass of ignorance was destroyed far too late. Cassie had paid the price when she was meant for so much more, but her life was cut too short. She ended it, but when no escape is seen from a life of pain after years of abuse, is it really her fault?

Circumstances brought the option into her mind. She proved actions have consequences and sometimes they are irreversible. Cassie was nothing, but another stolen life from abuse, bullying, and suicide.

People would now come to realize too late that their choices and cruel words did matter. Their blind eyes had impacted the course of events. It'd all led to an innocent's death. Regret will come to plague them to the end of their lives rather than if she'd lived.

Life would continue, but lives would come to be ruined.

Cassie

Dad's arms fall and my eyes once more wander over to my shattered body over the concrete. It hits me how real it all is. I'm dead.

I won't be in pain anymore. I'll no longer have to drown for the sake of others. Peace is an actual possibility. Happiness too.

But at what cost?

"They'll be okay, right daddy?" The question abandons me as my gaze is pulled once more by my loved ones. A sigh resonates in my ears.

"You shouldn't have ended your life so soon. It wasn't your time, my precious," he answers me and I shake my head as tears of grief abandon me.

Heartbreak is written all over those I love and I'm the

cause. I let them down. Broke them.

"I couldn't handle the pain anymore, daddy. Everyone kept hurting me and I just wanted it to stop. I didn't want to hurt anymore," I sob and his arms clasp around me tightly in comfort.

"I know my precious, but they couldn't hurt you anymore," he confesses, pulling me into his chest. "Your mom found out and set things right on your behalf. They're paying for the pain they brought you," he murmurs and my heart breaks.

"No one could hurt me anymore?"

Disbelief leads to an overwhelming pull of guilt and regret. My demons were gone. I didn't need to end it. I didn't need to hurt them.

"What happens now, daddy?"

He sighs again, and I feel crushed by the heavy weight of my head under the cold water. Fear slices through any peace and happiness that once filled me. Concern for those I left behind grows.

"None of them will ever be the same precious," he replies. "Their lives will continue on but they'll never know true happiness because they'll never be able to forget you. You'll live in them and your heartbreak will be their own."

"What does that mean?"

"Sadly, their lives will be met with great pains they won't be able to leave behind in the past that'll forever consume them."

"Because I ended my pain?"

"Your life was intertwined with theirs, my precious. By ending your life, you affected theirs. Thwarting them into alternative paths," he explains as tears bathe my cheeks.

"But they'll be okay?"

I'm met with silence.

"I broke them by ending my hell, didn't I?" I ask instead and he nods in sorrow.

"You had so much to do and so many lives to touch. You were meant to save many, but now..."

"What happens to me now?"

"You get to rest," he breathes, granting me a sliver of peace. "Your wings broke and you won't be able to aid all those you were destined to help, but he'll heal them for you. Your pure heart has granted you passage into paradise," he continues to speak, and my lips quiver. "You fell too soon."

"What about them? Will they get to rest?"

"In time, but come, you mustn't worry about them anymore. You'll watch over them and one day they'll come to join us," he tells me, slipping his hand into mine and walking me toward the light. Towards a place where the pain doesn't exist.

"I'm sorry," I whisper as I look back towards my loved ones once more, hoping I could take my choice back and wondering what life would have looked like had I stayed and fought.

Narrator

Cassie found peace alongside me, but it didn't minimize. She was a fallen angel that was seen far too late. Helped when she had already drowned and called it quits like so many other children.

People gathered around and saw her body lying there broken on the sidewalk, but eventually, they left too. Her family remained until they moved her, and it was a sight that left them forever marked. Cassie lived in a place free of pain that passed on to all those she left behind.

Liv became depressed and overly consumed by guilt that no doctor could cure. She passed away nearly a year after Cassie's death, unable to go on without her. Luisa and Luis Jr. were forced to live not only without their sister and father, but without their mother as well.

They were fortunate enough to have relatives take them in, but they ended up growing apart from one another. While their father spent the rest of his days in prison where he was eventually murdered for the abuse he inflicted on Cassie. The other inmates did not take kindly to his perversion towards young girls.

Becca succumbed to the clutches of addiction as she spiraled in her grief at losing her best friend. A few months later, she faced the death of her grandparents, who eventually lost to their illnesses. Her mother slipped into the grasp of alcoholism and down dangerous paths full of poor decisions.

One Beck followed as she sought to do everything to forget. Whether it be by alcohol or a high. Doing about anything to slip into momentary amnesia that always returned tenfold. Falling pregnant during one of her blackouts, but not even the hope of life growing in her womb, could get her to abandon her vice.

Instead, it further dove her into drowning as she was plagued with thoughts of Cassie and what-ifs. Eventually losing her life in an overdose two years after her best friend's death. Leaving her mother heartbroken and down a further spiral of addiction and loss.

Brad graduated high school and went off to college, but within the first year, he flushed out as he became a kindred spirit with alcohol. The sweet boy Cassie had met faded and morphed into a cold-hearted stranger who couldn't let anyone in. Broke too many hearts as he searched for her in every single woman he slept with.

Eventually left one pregnant and upon the discovery of the child, he went off and married her. Had a little girl who he named after his biggest love, much to her disarray, Cassandra. He dedicated his life to her and refused to have more children or even touch his wife, bringing her a life of misery, pain, and bitterness.

But by the time his daughter was in college, he developed cancer. His liver gave out on him when she was nineteen because of his years of severe drinking.

Luisa opened a foundation in the name of her sister with the help of her brother, but she never came to know happiness. Luis Jr. went on to have three children who he became estranged from and never got the chance to remedy. He eventually died in his late forties from a heart attack from too much stress.

The pain of the tragedy revolving around Cassie's death weighed heavily on them.

Her sister died alone at sixty, being remembered solely by those who she helped and saved. But it still was a dent compared to the lives Cassandra was meant to save. The world was not a better place without her.

All those that knew her carried her memory with them. She was never forgotten, unlike so many other children. No, she was used as an example while she watched everyone she loved wither away in misery without her.

The exact opposite of what she had expected. But it was too late to change her mind. Death cannot be undone. There is no reset button. No time machine in existence. So even amidst her peace, she regretted her choice.

Seeing the effects it had on everyone, she wished she'd never jumped.

Instead, she waited for all of them in paradise with open arms. None of them had genuine joy until they were reunited with her in death because she'd made the hard choice to end it all. They were robbed of different lives, filled with obstacles and joy. Condemned to live ones plagued with sorrow because, by the time everyone sought to help Cassie, it was too late to do anything.

Hugh went off to cross the lines of consent and came to be later arrested after becoming a serial rapist and raping six women. Two of which he left pregnant. All of them resembling Cassie, the girl he blamed for losing Becca and Jenine. A fate that devastated Jenine and left her further enveloped in a world of hate.

Her parents never did grow to accept her and blamed her for her brother's downfall. The second he was thrown into prison, they wrote the mean girl off. Jenine lost her sanity and was transferred to a mental institution where her eating disorders were discovered far too late as well. They claimed her life in a few short years.

Fanilea came to learn her victims' reality when she became fresh meat amongst other prisoners. Subjected to terrible hells, she could have never phantom. She continued to follow Jenine blindly until the queen bee was transferred away and eventually passed on to a better life.

She never met freedom again until her mid-forties, but by then her entire life had wasted away and Jenine was gone. She was alone and paying the consequences of making too many mistakes and ruining people's lives.

But Cassie's memory never left her either. After all, it had affected the world. Stricter bullying policies were created and the number of child abuse advocates came to grow. Everyone used her story as an example to save more lives. To break the silence.

Everyone knew of her. Of the life, she should have lived, but never got the chance to. A fallen angel that was unable to make the world a better place because death isn't the answer. Those lost are forever missed and deserved better, just as Cassie did.

So, please don't let angels fall. It's heartbreaking. Don't let lives be lost to the pain. Open your eyes and be aware of the signs. It could help save a life, just as Cassie's life could have been saved. Don't let children meet the same fate my daughter did.

An Angel

An angel fell on bushy thorns,
That pricked away at its feathers.
Its pain ignored by onlookers.
Until it was too late...
Its tears stained the ground.

¿FRIENDS?

Marked it in blood
As people passed by.
Left forgotten and broken
Another lost life.
With no one fighting for it.
No, they let it return to grace,
Way before it's time.
Because they chose blissful ignorance.
Instead of helping.
An angel fell and more continue to fall.
While most stand by,
As bystanders who peer,
But never aid.
When they should
Help mend broken wings.
Save a life,
And help an angel fly once more.
Don't let it fall,
Help it fly.
An angel is meant to soar
Through the heavenly blue skies.
Don't let it shed a tear.
They are not at fault
For the pain inflicted on them.
Help them survive,
From the cruelty.
They deserve to smile
Feel nothing but joy.
They shouldn't be drowned in sorrow.
So, help an angel fly.
Don't let it fall
Because angels are meant to soar
Through the heavenly blue skies.

Grace Wins

♥

Cassie

MY EYES CLOSE AS my descent to death begins. The wind slaps against my skin. This is it. I'm going to die. Abandon this world to flee to one without pain.

A deathly grip clings to my skin and I hiss at the pain as my body swings against the side of the building. My eyelids snap open and as my gaze travels up, I'm met with a woman bearing a determined stare. Her upper body leans out the window as she holds me for dear life.

Preventing my fall. Keeping me from freedom and anchored to the pain. I try to wrestle myself free, but it's an impossible task. Her grasp is unwavering and fierce.

"Hold on! I got you," she calls out and tears swell up, burning at my retinas. They stream down and bathe my cheeks as I plead, through a look, with her. Doing nothing to hide my agony. Hoping she takes mercy on me and lets me go.

Whispers and rustling travel through the wind into my ears and fear trickles through my heart. Without the need for words, I already know I've lost this battle. I'm going to be forced to continue being tethered to a life of suffering and silence.

Another arm clasps tightly around us both and I'm pulled up to face the illusion of safety in the form of a hospital room.

But that's something I've never had. Perhaps my body will be free from injury in their eyes, but it won't last. My mind is gone, and my tormentors will mark my flesh with blows the second I leave this building.

I know it. But it seems I can't escape it.

"Why can't you let me die?" I breathe out, drawing my knees to my chest. "Can't you see I don't want to live?" The question tumbles out in sobs, I hope, breaks their hearts as much as mine. "I can't go back to that hell. I want to stop hurting."

"Your stepfather?" She questions me and my distress only grows. She knows and yet she kept me from abandoning the cruel world that is dead set on breaking me over and over.

I nod as hope trickles through my blood. Maybe admitting it will rid me of the agony. Perhaps destroying the silence will get them to set me free. Unbind me from the pain.

"Cassie, your stepfather was arrested the day after you were admitted," a gruff voice says in the softest of tones. My hope dies instantly at his lies. "Your mother found your diary and reported him to the authorities," he adds, but his words are too sweet and good to be true.

"He's rotting in jail where he belongs," her voice filters through and I dare to glance over at her while slapping my tears away, wishing to see her eyes. My gaze locks with hers and I try to unearth the truth in her blue-gray irises, but there's no sign of deception.

Maybe she's telling the truth, or she's a good liar. People lie all the time. Some to harm and others to protect.

"You've been in a coma for months now," the man speaks next to the woman. He catches my attention in his white coat and I hold my breath in hopes he'll tell me more. Doctors can't lie, can they?

"Your mom found out about the bullying you've been subjected to and reported it both to the school and authorities," the woman speaks again and a shiver takes over me. Cold seeps deep into my bones at the thought of my worst fear coming to life. Being the cause of my family's pain and the one to break them.

"Most of the school was sentenced to community service. Others were put under house arrest. A few were expelled and charged with assault," she explains. "They discovered you were pushed off your balcony and the two responsible are locked behind bars."

"You have nothing to fear. No one will hurt you anymore," he adds, and my heart shatters at his words. They're the ones I've always wanted to hear, but I can't believe them. They're too pretty to be real.

Life doesn't like me. No one does. I'm nothing but their punching bag. Paying for every broken plate.

Both their eyes bleed with sincerity, but I can't believe them. My retinas burn as tears once more flood out and pour mercilessly over my cheeks.

"Here, look," she says gifting me her phone, inspiring my confusion. "It's been all over the news," she explains, and I reach for it with trembling hands. Desperate for proof of the truth.

Shock instills in my brain as I tap through the multitude of articles tied to my name. My fingers scroll through everything, reading every single word. My heart fearing it to be a ruse like the last email I received.

I find every word the doctors said to be true. My stepfather was sentenced to thirty-six years in prison for every one of his blows and raping me. Jenine and Fanilea were condemned to over eighteen years behind bars for taking things too far and pushing me off the railing.

Articles about me and my hell *everywhere.* The media keeping up with my recovery. Detailing me being in a coma for over ten months with my mother refusing to pull the plug. People setting up funds to pay for my hospital bills.

A news story title catches my attention and my heart stops. **Becca Jones, a key witness in Jenine Squire's Trial**. My finger taps on it before I can even second guess and scrolls through every bit of information available. My lungs contract as a video appears and I click play.

"Cassie is my best friend, and I let her down. I chose popularity over her, and I regret it so much..." Becks cries. *"I wish I could turn back time... but I can't. I can only spend the rest of my life making up for my mistakes, starting now by helping one of her tormentors go to jail no matter how much it hurts. So that when she wakes up, she can be proud of me. Like I know she'll be when she finds out she inspires me to pursue a degree in criminology so I can help as many as I can."*

My finger presses pause for a brief second as grief overwhelms me. But I breathe in deeply and resume watching. Needing the slightest of signs to see that my best friend might not be lost.

"Because she's a true angel, and she'll forever be my best friend, even if I'll never gain her forgiveness. Cassie is the best parts of me and I will be better for her like she deserves. I'll be brave and break the silence."

The video ends and I weep at her words. Becks, my best friend, doesn't hate me. She loves me. Chose me over Jenine.

My tormentors can hurt me no more.

Whimpers escape me as I wail and crumble at the change of events. My shackles are now gone, but the marks remain. I thought the pain would disappear when they did, but I'm still in pain. My insides still bleed and my will to live is nonexistent.

The doctors' arms wrap around me as I fall apart.

My tormentors are paying for their crimes, but they haven't left me. They continue to live rent-free in my head. I'm *free* of *them,* but not the agony they instilled me with.

Regret should be running rampant through my veins at the thought that I almost ended everything when they are already paying for their crime. But it doesn't.

I'm free, yet I'm not.

Narrator

Cassandra was referred to a psychiatrist later in the day to determine the best course of action for her to heal because despite her body being better; her mind, heart, and soul were not. Her demons were physically out of her life, but she had endless trauma to work on that wouldn't go away overnight. Perhaps never.

But with time, she could come to learn to deal and live with it. She did as she was transferred to a retreat where others like her could go on the mend. For her well-being, those she loved were not allowed to visit, but were informed of her progress.

It broke their hearts, but they understood.

For four months, Cassie spent her days in therapy, group activities, and getting her high school diploma. When she was released, she returned home, not cured, but better. Ready to take on the world; with an arsenal of healthy coping mechanisms and tips.

It was all that they could all ask for as they greeted her with a fresh start.

Her old family home sold, and her new one far away from it. A one story with an acre of land. But one she loved as much as her family.

Becca and Cassie reconciled and truly became the best of friends, with both of them becoming truly inseparable. My precious being utterly proud of her for being enrolled in college and pursuing her criminology degree. Becks helped her apply to college and helped her with financial aid applications.

In time, she was accepted into an Ivy League university with a full ride, where she pursued a degree in psychology.

Long forgetting her previous plan and following her heart. As she did with Brad, who had also waited for her with open arms and the two began dating as she began the new chapter of her life.

But not long after Cassie began classes, Becca's grandparents passed away from their medical issues. Devastation met them and Becks's was left to answer for a pile of debt as her mother was further consumed by alcohol. She nearly lost herself, if not for Cassie being by her side.

Together, they got her mother into rehab to get the help she needed and moved into an apartment near Becca's school. And upon receiving her inheritance from my death, my precious cleared her best friend's debt and paid for her education. Wanting Becks to succeed in life and allowing Becca from transferring out to her chosen university sooner.

Still, from time to time, as they both pursued different degrees in different universities, they would do semesters abroad to see more of the world. Both always keeping in contact and sharing all the details of their experiences. With Brad wholeheartedly supporting Cassie every step of the way.

His love for her never wavering and only growing as he saw her become the person she was always meant to be. Happy. So, he happily waited for her every time and allowed her to set the pace of their relationship. Being a true gentleman like every man should be with the one they love.

And near graduation, Cassandra gained the courage to face Jenine after hearing bits and pieces of her story from Becca. Together, both friends traveled to the prison to see the mean girl, who showed Cassie nothing but hostility until Becks stepped in. Soon after, my precious learned about Jenine's entire story.

None of which excused the pain she inflicted on others, but it made Cassie understand what led her to it.

Both of them continued to visit Jenine and with time the queen bee came to overcome her hate and get help. It was there that doctors discovered her eating disorders, and she could finally get treatment for it. Cassie quit going but kept up to date with news about her through Becca, who became the friend Jeni needed to be better.

After all, deep down, the mean girl was simply a girl in dire need of her parents' love and approval. Hurting others because she was hurting. People truly handle difficulties in different ways.

Eventually, both friends walked across different stages with college diplomas in hand. Becca became a probation officer, wanting to help others rectify their past mistakes and become better versions of themselves. Meanwhile, Cassie pursued higher education as she became a licensed therapist to help as many as she could.

Brad proposed shortly after Cassandra's graduation and a few short months later they married in a small intimate wedding with simply loved ones in attendance. Becca came to meet a social worker shortly after and married him within a year and a half of meeting him with Cassie's blessing. Not long after the wedding, they welcomed a daughter into the world and named her in my daughter's honor.

Unfortunately, not long after the birth, Becca faced the discovery of a malignant tumor growing in her womb. A long battle with cancer began, but with everyone's support, she came to kick cancer's ass. Sadly, she was unable to have any more biological children, but later on came to adopt a pair of siblings that left their family complete.

Olivia remained single throughout it all and dedicated her life to her children and came to open her own business. Later on, with Becca and Cassie's help, she started a foundation to help as many abused children as she could. Which ultimately helped many.

Regardless of her personal feelings toward Luis Anas, she still took their kids to visit them because, despite the hurt he inflicted on Cassie, not once did it extend to them. As much as he had hurt their older sister, they still loved him greatly.

They were unable to forget the good times and visited him without fail for ten years before he lost his life in a prison riot trying to escape.

Both siblings were left devastated and his son developed a drinking problem, but with time was able to overcome it with the help and support of his family. In time, he became a world-renowned soccer player with a mechanical engineering degree. Meanwhile, Luisa dove into her studies and became a lawyer in honor of both Cassie and her father, who always encouraged her to pursue a law degree.

Hugh visited both his sister and Fanilea without fail for years, eventually falling in love with Fani, and despite her being behind bars; the pair got married. But he developed a nasty habit of drugs and passed away from a drug overdose before she was released.

Brad and my precious traveled for a bit as she became a very well-known child abuse advocate and therapist that helped people who were struggling. Even going as far as writing a book detailing her hell and healing journey in hopes it would help others. Giving away as many copies as she could for free as she found it pure nonsense to charge survivors for something that could help them.

In her spare time, she continued to paint and, from persuasion from both her husband and best friend, she came to sell her art. Donating all proceeds to her mother's foundation.

Both she and Brad sought to settle down and have a family and welcomed their first child two years before he left his job as an operations research analyst for a renowned company to begin his own. And during those two years, Cassie became a stay-at-home mom to enjoy the little precious moments of their firsts.

By the time Jenine was released from prison in her late thirties, she was a reformed woman and Cassandra was a mother to four. The mean girl came to meet a teacher and married her without a care for anyone's acceptance, having finally accepted herself. So despite her parents not going, her happiness didn't diminish.

However, Cassie and Becca attended both the ceremony and reception.

Everyone reaped what they sowed in time. Becca came to learn the true meaning of friendship and never let it go. Jenine repented and learned hate could easily kill as well as it kept one from happiness. Cassie came to change the world for the better because she got help and could be saved in time.

The world came to know their story and learn the horrifying choices and effects bullying, child abuse, and suicide could have on a child. They learned bullies typically lashed out from a place of hurt because they, too, were or were being hurt. Not to mention they came to learn the power of friendship and its meaning.

My precious Cassandra Castillo was a true angel at heart who came to save any lives with both her words and actions. She inspired many to act because ignorance and silence weren't bliss but hell. Both those things cost lives, and death wasn't something that could be undone.

Lives could be saved if people spoke out, and they too could learn, just like Cassie, that **grace wins** every time if one keeps fighting.

Parting Words

Cassie

I WAS A BROKEN girl who had enough and became a fallen angel. Gave up on life after agonizing hardships and in the end, did what I never sought to do. Hurt the ones I love the most. Ending it was the hardest choice I ever made.

Even if others had never suggested it, I would have come to it on my own. I was far too gone by the time the world found out the truth. Being subjected to the silence spared others from pain for mere seconds, but my death left them with a gaping hole I honestly regret.

I wish I could have held on and seen that grace wins but I couldn't. The pain was far too much for me to see the other side. I refused to listen and subject myself to and for the sake of others because I was too selfless. That is something I'll never regret.

Putting others before me.

But what I do regret is never realizing that I couldn't save anyone if I didn't save myself first. Perhaps if I'd spoken out, then I wouldn't be dead and I could have soared through the skies aiding others like me. But that was not my story.

Regardless of my story, I wish those in pain find their own grace wins happy ending.

So here we are on the outskirts of paradise overlooking the world below, uttering our last parting words in the hope they might save someone. Wishing that perhaps we'll break the veil between life and death, even if I know it's not possible. Still, I yearn for it.

"If you're at the mercy of others and agonizing, stay strong. You aren't alone, and it's okay to seek help. Silence kills far too much than many will ever tell you. You deserve to smile and be happy," the words slip past my lips and into the wind that I hope find their way to those who need them.

"Don't stay in an abusive relationship, and speak out in dangerous situations. Sometimes those around won't catch the signs of your distress till it's too late. Don't become a fallen angel like my precious did. You deserve a happy ending as much as she did," dad speaks to my right and my soul aches.

He was my guardian angel, and I let him down by joining him before my time.

"Let the authorities and adults know when you're being hurt so they may do something. Because everyone deserves a life free of pain. Everyone might not believe you, but someone will, and that's all you need. Don't seek to escape the torment in the arms of death. You'll only let the monsters win," mom says to my left.

"Everyone's life matters, and I wish I knew that sooner," Jenine voices with a clogged throat. After all, it took her a long time before she found peace in paradise, having to atone somewhere else for her wrongs. "I wish I hadn't tormented many and became their nightmare. That I hadn't become a monster... no matter how much you hurt, don't become like those that hurt you. The damage never goes away."

"Child abuse, bullying, and suicide are not topics to be taken lightly," Brad remarks behind me as his arms wrap around my waist and his head rests over my own. A bitter-sweet smile crosses my face. We were meant to live a different life together and my choice ruined that. "If you're its victim, say something, please."

"Adults are sometimes blind, and won't see the truth till there's nothing they can't do, and sometimes not even then. But don't let that stop you from screaming it to the four winds, because you're a survivor, not a victim," Luisa adds next to mom.

"Be strong, kind, and courageous," Becca shares next. "Find out who your genuine friends are and hold on tight to them while you weed out the fake ones. Friendship is everything, and trust means more than a thousand words. Don't break it. If you mess up, apologize and make it up to them. Be there for them as they will be for you, and if they're hurt with you by their side, help them gain the courage they need to shatter their silence. Don't rob them of their story."

I reach out for her hand and give it a gentle squeeze. We lost our way in life, but found it back to one another in death. Because we truly were best friends. Sad: we became inseparable when our souls reunited in paradise, and couldn't do so on Earth.

"And one day you'll come to live your own love story. It may happen at the oddest of times and most unexpected of ways, but it'll happen. So, don't let your abusers keep you from it by keeping silent," Brad argues, and a laugh escapes me. Only he would want people to find love and live their own fairytale or as close as they can.

"You deserve a life of joy and sure life is unfair. You'll face trials, but happiness still exists out there. Onlookers, if you see something, do something. Far too many lives are lost, hoping for the best. Don't let fear allow you to ignore a cry for help. So step in or get the necessary attention to the situation. A life can be saved," Luis Junior chimes in with words instilled with hope.

"Be brave, speak up, and dream. It's hard, but worth it. You matter and help exists, so face the fear, and be a little selfish by breaking the silence. You can't help anyone if you don't save yourself first. It'll leave you one step closer to your happy ending," I complete with dire hope to instill these

words into the many.

My story has to be worth something to someone. I may not have gotten to tell it in life, but maybe, just maybe, it'll reach someone and save at least one. So they may know grace wins and change the lives of many with their smiles.

"Let's go rest," dad says. "We've said our parting words and we can only hope for the best now, my precious," he adds and I simply nod before fully embracing a life of peace with those I love most.

Acknowledgments

♥

First, I would like to thank two of my closest friends for being there for me during my most difficult times back when I was 15. I truly do not know where I would be if not for them. So, sincerely, Beatriz and Jessica, know you mean the world to me. I would also like to thank my mother for always supporting me and being my biggest cheerleader, which is more than I can ask for. Last, I would like to thank all those who have supported me and believed in me to get here.

And the biggest shout out to two exceptional souls who, unbeknownst to them, kept me going forward so I could become who I am today. My communities in schools coordinators from high school; Ellen Leder and Ute Rowe. From the bottom of my heart, thank you for everything you did for me.

Thank you for encouraging me to follow my dreams.

Of course, I can't forget my soulmate for cheering me on, and having great faith in me. The world is not ready for all the crazy we'll craft together, and I honestly can't wait till we begin co-writing.

I first wrote this story when I was sixteen and my mental health was in pieces. Now, seven years later, it's a full-length novel. It's a full circle and poetic for ¿Friends? to be the first book, I publish, but perfect at the same time.

Cassie was born during some of my most painful moments. She came to me, shared her story, and insisted on me sharing it with the world so she could bring awareness and save as many lives as possible. Seeking to do so by letting the hurt know they aren't alone and their pain is valid while inspiring those in ignorance to help.

So thank you for supporting us both by reading her story. If you happen to be in Cassie's shoes, a person being hurt by others, know my heart goes out to you. More so, I want you to know you are loved and worthy of everything good in this world. Stay strong and know both she and I wish you to have the happy ending she deserved. Please don't be afraid to reach out for help. Happiness is possible.

Had Cassie done so, it would have gone differently. Don't be discouraged, someone will listen, and if they refuse to, then scream even louder. Put yourself first. Fight for yourself if no one else does. You hold far more value than you may give yourself credit for and those that love you see that. Better yet, they'll remind you, and if they put you down, then leave them behind because they don't deserve you.

Never lower your expectations and don't settle for less or the bare minimum, because you deserve the world. Your happy ending will come. Simply take the first step and break the silence. Those that hurt us always prefer to keep us in silence because it keeps them in power. Don't. Speak out and live your best life. That'll always be the best revenge against them.

About the Author

C.H. Magical is an artsy soul who has a profound love to create all sorts of wonders. For years, her passion has been writing and crafting both stories and art that others can relate to and love. Dabbling in about just every genre because she loves the challenge.

When she isn't off somewhere plotting and typing a brand new idea despite the many drafts she harbors already, she can be found doing numerous other things. Such as traveling to other lands and falling in love with swoon-worthy men in books. Painting and sketching whenever her heart finds inspiration. Or she'll simply be spending time with family and friends because she knows every moment counts.

All the while, deep down, she dreams of sparking a change, no matter how small in the world for it to become better. She seeks to spread love through every painting, sketch, poem, song, story, novel; everything she creates. Because she knows that in times of need, a work of art can be all someone needs to heal and to know they aren't alone.

www.ingramcontent.com/pod-product-compliance
Lightning Source LLC
Chambersburg PA
CBHW060619310726
48982CB00003B/608

* 9 7 9 8 9 8 8 0 2 9 9 2 2 *